Mercier and Camier

WORKS BY SAMUEL BECKETT PUBLISHED BY GROVE PRESS

Collected Poems in English and French

The Collected Shorter Plays
(All That Fall, Act Without Words I, Act Without Words II, Krapp's Last Tape, Rough for Theatre I, Rough for Theatre II, Embers, Rough for Radio I, Rough for Radio II, Words and Music, Cascando, Play, Film, The Old Tune, Come and Go, Eh Joe, Breath, Not I, That Time, Footfalls, Ghost Trio, . . . but the clouds . . . , A Piece of Monologue, Rockaby, Ohio Impromptu, Quad, Catastrophe, Nacht and Träume, What Where)

The Complete Short Prose: 1929–1989
(Assumption, Sedendo et Quiescendo, Text, A Case in a Thousand, First Love, The Expelled, The Calmative, The End, Texts for Nothing 1–13, From an Abandoned Work, The Image, All Strange Away, Imagination Dead Imagine, Enough, Ping, Lessness, The Lost Ones, Fizzles 1–8, Heard in the Dark 1, Heard in the Dark 2, One Evening, As the story was told, The Cliff, neither, Stirrings Still, Variations on a "Still" Point, *Faux Départs*, The Capital of the Ruins)

Disjecta: Miscellaneous Writings and a Dramatic Fragment

Endgame and Act Without Words

Ends and Odds

First Love and Other Shorts

Happy Days

How It Is

I Can't Go On, I'll Go On: A Samuel Beckett Reader

Krapp's Last Tape
(All That Fall, Embers, Act Without Words I, Act Without Words II)

Mercier and Camier

Molloy

More Pricks Than Kicks
(Dante and the Lobster, Fingal, Ding-Dong, A Wet Night, Love and Lethe, Walking Out, What a Misfortune, The Smeraldina's Billet Doux, Yellow, Draff)

Murphy

Nohow On
(Company, Ill Seen Ill Said, Worstward Ho)

The Poems, Short Fiction, and Criticism of Samuel Beckett

Rockaby and Other Short Plays
(Rockaby, Ohio Impromptu, All Strange Away, and A Piece of Monologue)

The Selected Works of Samuel Beckett
(boxed paperback set)
Volume I: Novels
(Murphy, Watt, Mercier and Camier)
Volume II: Novels
(Molloy, Malone Dies, The Unnamable, How It Is)
Volume III: Dramatic Works
Volume IV: Poems, Short Fiction, Criticism

Stories and Texts for Nothing
(The Expelled, The Calmative, The End, Texts for Nothing 1–13)

Three Novels
(Molloy, Malone Dies, The Unnamable)

Waiting for Godot

Waiting for Godot: A Bilingual Edition

Watt

Samuel Beckett

Mercier and Camier

Grove Press
New York

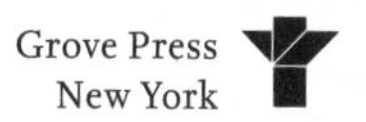

Originally published in French in 1970 by
Les Éditions de Minuit, Paris, under the title *Mercier et Camier.*

First published in the author's translation in 1974
in Great Britain by Calder & Boyars Ltd., London.

The first Grove Press edition was published in 1975.

Design, composition, and textual supervision by Laura Lindgren

Printed in the United States of America

Library of Congress Catalog Card Number: 74-21639

ISBN 978-0-8021-4444-7

Grove Press
an imprint of Grove/Atlantic, Inc.
841 Broadway
New York, NY 10003

DISTRIBUTED BY PUBLISHERS GROUP WEST
WWW.GROVEATLANTIC.COM

11 12 13 14 15 10 9 8 7 6 5 4 3 2 1

Mercier and Camier

I

The journey of Mercier and Camier is one I can tell, if I will, for I was with them all the time.

Physically it was fairly easy going, without seas or frontiers to be crossed, through regions untormented on the whole, if desolate in parts. Mercier and Camier did not remove from home, they had that great good fortune. They did not have to face, with greater or less success, outlandish ways, tongues, laws, skies, foods, in surroundings little resembling those to which first childhood, then boyhood, then manhood had inured them. The weather, though often inclement (but they knew no better), never exceeded the limits of the temperate, that is to say of what could still be borne, without danger if not without discomfort, by the average native fittingly clad and shod. With regard to money, if it did not run to first class transport or the palatial hotel, still there was enough to keep them going, to and fro, without recourse to alms. It may be said therefore that in this respect too they were fortunate, up to a point. They had to struggle, but less than many must, less perhaps than most of those who venture forth, driven by a need now clear and now obscure.

They had consulted together at length, before embarking on this journey, weighing with all the calm at their command what benefits they might hope from it, what ills apprehend, maintaining turn about the dark side and the rosy. The only certitude they gained from these debates was that of not lightly launching out, into the unknown.

Camier was first to arrive at the appointed place. That is to say that on his arrival Mercier was not there. In reality Mercier had forestalled him by a good ten minutes. Not Camier then, but Mercier, was first to arrive. He possessed himself in patience for five minutes, with his eye on the various avenues of approach open to his friend, then set out for a saunter destined to last full fifteen minutes. Meantime Camier, five minutes having passed without sight or sign of Mercier, took himself off in his turn for a little stroll. On his return to the place, fifteen minutes later, it was in vain he cast about him, and understandably so. For Mercier, after cooling his heels for a further five minutes, had wandered off again for what he pleased to call a little stretch. Camier hung around for five more minutes, then again departed, saying to himself, Perhaps I'll run into him in the street. It was at this moment that Mercier, back from his breather, which as chance this time would have it had not exceeded ten minutes, glimpsed receding in the morning mist a shape suggestive of Camier's and which was indeed none other. Unhappily it vanished as though swallowed up by the cobbles, leaving Mercier to resume his vigil. But on expiry of what is beginning to look like the regulation five minutes he abandoned it again, feeling the need of a little motion. Their joy was thus for an instant unbounded, Mercier's joy and Camier's joy, when after five and ten minutes respectively of uneasy prowl, debouching simultaneously on the square, they found themselves face to face for the first time since the evening before. The time was nine fifty in the morning.

In other words:

	Arr.	Dep.	Arr.	Dep.	Arr.	Dep.	Arr.
Mercier	9:05	9:10	9:25	9:30	9:40	9:45	9:50
Camier	9:15	9:20	9:35	9:40	9:50		

What stink of artifice.

They were still in each other's arms when the rain began to fall, with quite oriental abruptness. They made therefore with all speed to the shelter which, in the form of a pagoda, had been erected here as protection from the rain and other inclemencies, in a word from the weather. Shadowy and abounding in nooks and crannies it was a friend to lovers also and to the aged of either sex. Into this refuge, at the same instant as our heroes, bounded a dog, followed shortly by a second. Mercier and Camier, irresolute, exchanged a look. They had not finished in each other's arms and yet felt awkward about resuming. The dogs for their part were already copulating, with the utmost naturalness.

The place where they now found themselves, where they had agreed, not without pains, that they should meet, was not properly speaking a square, but rather a small public garden at the heart of a tangle of streets and lanes. It displayed the usual shrubberies, flower-beds, pools, fountains, statues, lawns and benches in strangulating profusion. It had something of the maze, irksome to perambulate, difficult of egress, for one not in its secrets. Entry was of course the simplest thing in the world. In the centre, roughly, towered huge a shining copper beech, planted several centuries earlier, according to the sign rudely nailed to the bole, by a Field Marshal of France peacefully named Saint-Ruth. Hardly had he done so, in the words of the inscription, when he was struck dead by a cannon-ball, faithful to the last to the same hopeless cause, on a battlefield having little in common, from the point of view of landscape, with those on which he had won his spurs, first as brigadier, then as lieutenant, if that is the order in which spurs are won, on the battlefield. It was no doubt to this tree that the garden owed its existence, a consequence which can scarcely have occurred to the Field Marshal as on that distant day, well clear of the quincunxes, before an elegant and replete assistance, he held the frail sapling upright in the hole gorged with evening dew. But to have done with this tree and hear no more about it, from it the garden derived what little charm it still possessed, not to mention of course its name. The stifled giant's days were numbered, it would not cease henceforward to pine and rot till finally removed, bit by bit. Then for a while, in the garden mysteriously named, people would breathe more freely.

Mercier and Camier did not know the place. Hence no doubt their choice of it for their meeting. Certain things shall never be known for sure.

Through the orange panes the rain to them seemed golden and brought back memories, determined by the hazard of their excursions, to the one of Rome, of Naples to the other, mutually unavowed and with a feeling akin to shame. They should have felt the better for this glow of distant days when they were young, and warm, and loved art, and mocked marriage, and did not know each other, but they felt no whit the better.

Let us go home, said Camier.

Why? said Mercier.

It won't stop all day, said Camier.

Long or short, tis but a shower, said Mercier.

I can't stand there doing nothing, said Camier.

Then let us sit, said Mercier.

Worse still, said Camier.

Then let us walk up and down, said Mercier, yes, arm in arm let us pace to and fro. There is not much room, but there might be even less. Lay down our umbrella, there, help me off with our knapsack, so, thanks, and off we go.

Camier submitted.

Every now and then the sky lightened and the rain abated. Then they would halt before the door. This was the signal for the sky to darken again and the rain to redouble in fury.

Don't look, said Mercier.

The sound is enough, said Camier.

True, said Mercier.

After a moment of silence Mercier said:

The dogs don't trouble you?

Why does he not withdraw? said Camier.

He cannot, said Mercier.

Why? said Camier.

One of nature's little gadgets, said Mercier, no doubt to make insemination double sure.

They begin astraddle, said Camier, and finish arsy-versy.

What would you? said Mercier. The ecstasy is past, they yearn to part, to go and piss against a post or eat a morsel of shit, but cannot. So they turn their backs on each other. You'd do as much, if you were they.

Delicacy would restrain me, said Camier.

And what would you do? said Mercier.

Feign regret, said Camier, that I could not renew such pleasure incontinent.

After a moment of silence Camier said:

Let us sit us down, I feel all sucked off.

You mean sit down, said Mercier.

I mean sit us down, said Camier.

Then let us sit us down, said Mercier.

On all hands already the workers were at it again, the air waxed loud with cries of pleasure and pain and with the urbaner notes of those for whom life had exhausted its surprises, as well on the minus side as on the plus. Things too were getting ponderously under way. It was in vain the rain poured down, the whole business was starting again with apparently no less ardour than if the sky had been a cloudless blue.

You kept me waiting, said Mercier.

On the contrary, said Camier.

I arrived at nine five, said Mercier.

And I at nine fifteen, said Camier.

You see, said Mercier.

Waiting, said Camier, and keeping waiting can only be with reference to a pre-arranged terminus.

And for what hour was our appointment, according to you? said Mercier.

Nine fifteen, said Camier.

Then you are grievously mistaken, said Mercier.

Meaning? said Camier.

Will you never have done astounding me? said Mercier.

Explain yourself, said Camier.

I close my eyes and live it over again, said Mercier, your hand in mine, tears rising to my eyes and the sound of my faltering voice, So be it, tomorrow at nine. A drunken woman passed by, singing a ribald song and hitching up her skirts.

She went to your head, said Camier. He took a notebook from his pocket, turned the leaves and read: Monday 15, St. Macanus, 9:15, St. Ruth, collect umbrella at Helen's.

And what does that prove? said Mercier.

My good faith, said Camier.

True, said Mercier.

We shall never know, said Camier, at what hour we arranged to meet today, so let us drop the subject.

In all this confusion one thing alone is sure, said Mercier, and that is that we met at ten to ten, at the same time as the hands, or rather a moment later.

There is that to be thankful for, said Camier.

The rain had not yet begun, said Mercier.

The morning fervour was intact, said Camier.

Don't lose our agenda, said Mercier.

At this moment suddenly appeared from nowhere the first of a long line of maleficent beings. His uniform, sickly green in colour, its place of honour rife with heroic emblems and badges, suited him down to the ground. Inspired by the example of the great Sarsfield he had risked his life without success in defence of a territory which in itself must have left him cold and considered as a symbol cannot have greatly heated him either. He carried a stick at once elegant and massive and even leaned on it from time to time. He suffered torment with his hip, the pain shot down his buttock and up his rectum deep into the bowels and even as far north as the pyloric valve, culminating as a matter of course in uretro-scrotal spasms with quasi-incessant longing to micturate. Invalided out with a grudging pension, whence the sour looks of nearly all those, male and female, with whom his duties and remnants of bonhomie brought him daily in contact, he sometimes felt it would have been wiser on his part, during the great upheaval, to devote his energies to the domestic skirmish, the Gaelic dialect, the fortification of his faith and the treasures of a folklore beyond compare. The bodily danger would have been less and the benefits more certain. But this thought, when he had relished all its bitterness, he would banish from his mind, as unworthy of it. His moustache, once stiff as the lip it was grown to hide, was no longer so. From time to time, when he remembered, with a blast from below of fetid breath mingled with spittle, he straightened it momentarily. Motionless at the foot of the pagoda steps, his cape agape, streaming with rain, he darted his eyes to and fro, from Mercier and Camier to the dogs, from the dogs to Mercier and Camier.

Who owns that bicycle? he said.

Mercier and Camier exchanged a look.

We could have done without this, said Camier.

Shift her, said the ranger.

It may prove diverting, said Mercier.

Who owns them dogs? said the ranger.

I don't see how we can stay, said Camier.

Can it I wonder be the fillip we needed, to get us moving? said Mercier.

The ranger mounted the steps of the shelter and stood stock still in the doorway. The air darkened immediately and turned a deeper yellow.

I think he is about to attack us, said Camier.

I leave the balls to you, as usual, said Mercier.

Dear sergeant, said Camier, what exactly can we do for you?

You see that bicycle? said the ranger.

I see nothing, said Camier. Mercier, do you see a bicycle?

Is she yours? said the ranger.

A thing we do not see, said Camier, for whose existence we have only your word, how are we to tell if it is ours, or another's?

Why would it be ours? said Mercier. Are these dogs ours? No. We see them today for the first time. And you would have it that the bicycle, assuming it exists, is ours? And yet the dogs are not ours.

Bugger the dogs, said the ranger.

But as if to give himself the lie he fell on them with stick and boot and drove them cursing from the pagoda. Tied together as they still were, by the post-coitus, their retreat was no easy matter. For the efforts they made to escape, acting equally in opposite directions, could not but annul each other. They must have greatly suffered.

He has now buggered the dogs, said Mercier.

He has driven them from the shelter, said Camier, there is no denying that, but by no means from the garden.

The rain will soon wash them loose, said Mercier. Less rut-besotted they would have thought of it themselves.

The fact is he has done them a service, said Camier.

Let us show him a little kindness, said Mercier, he's a hero of the great war. Here we were, high and dry, masturbating full pelt without fear of interruption, while he was crawling in the Flanders mud, shitting in his puttees.

Conclude nothing from those idle words, Mercier and Camier were old young.

It's an idea, said Camier.

Will you look at that clatter of decorations, said Mercier. Do you realize the gallons of diarrhoea that represents?

Darkly, said Camier, as only one so costive can.

Let us suppose this alleged bicycle is ours, said Mercier. Where lies the harm?

A truce to dissembling, said Camier, it is ours.

Shift her out of here, said the ranger.

The day has dawned at last, said Camier, after years of shilly-shally, when we must go, we know not whither, perhaps never to return . . . alive. We are simply waiting for the day to lift, then full speed ahead. Try and understand.

What is more, said Mercier, we have still thought to take, before it is too late.

Thought to take? said Camier.

Those were my words, said Mercier.

I thought all thought was taken, said Camier, and all in order.

All is not, said Mercier.

Will you shift her or won't you? said the ranger.

Are you venal, said Mercier, since you are deaf to reason?

Silence.

Can you be bought off? said Mercier.

Certainly, said the ranger.

Give him a bob, said Mercier. To think our first disbursement should be a sop to bribery and extortion.

The ranger vanished with a curse.

How of a piece they all are, said Mercier.

Now he'll prowl around, said Camier.

What can that matter to us? said Mercier.

I don't like being prowled around, said Camier.

Mercier took exception to this turn. Camier maintained it. This little game soon palled. It must have been near noon.

And now, said Mercier, the time is come for us.

For us? said Camier.

Precisely, said Mercier, for us, for serious matters.

What about a bite to eat? said Camier.

Thought first, said Mercier, then sustenance.

A long debate ensued, broken by long silences in which thought took place. At such times they would sink, now Mercier, now Camier, to such depths of meditation that the voice of one, resuming its drift, was powerless to bring the other back, or passed unheard. Or they would arrive simultaneously at often contrary conclusions and simultaneously begin to state them. Nor was it rare for one to lapse into a brood before the other had concluded his exposé. And there were times they would look long at each other, unable to utter a word, their minds two blanks. It was fresh from one such daze they decided to abandon their enquiry, for the time being. The afternoon was well advanced, the rain was falling still, the short winter day was drawing to a close.

It is you have the provisions, said Mercier.

On the contrary, said Camier.

True, said Mercier.

My hunger is gone, said Camier.

One must eat, said Mercier.

I see no point, said Camier.

We have a long hard road before us still, said Mercier.

The sooner we drop the better, said Camier.

True, said Mercier.

The ranger's head appeared in the doorway. Believe it or not, only his head was to be seen. It was to say, in his quaint way, they were free to spend the night for half-a-crown.

Is thought now taken, said Camier, and all in order?

No, said Mercier.

Will all ever be? said Camier.

I believe so, said Mercier, yes, I believe, not firmly, no, but I believe, yes, the day is coming when all will be in order, at last.

That will be delightful, said Camier.

Let us hope so, said Mercier.

A long look passed between them. Camier said to himself, Even him I cannot see. A like thought agitated his vis-à-vis.

Two points seemed nevertheless established as a result of this consultation.

1. Mercier would set off alone, awheel, with the raincoat. Wherever he should stop for the night, at the first stage, he would get all in readiness to receive Camier. Camier would take the road as soon as the weather permitted. Camier would keep the umbrella. No mention of the sack.

2. It so chanced that Mercier, up to now, had shown himself the live wire, Camier the dead weight. The reverse was to be expected at any moment. On the less weak let the weaker always lean, for the course to follow. They might conceivably be valiant together. That would be the day. Or the great weakness might overtake them simultaneously. Let them in this case not give way to despair, but wait with confidence for the evil moment to pass. In spite of the vagueness of these expressions they understood each other, more or less.

Not knowing what to think, said Camier, I look away.

It would seem to be lifting, said Mercier.

The sun comes out at last, said Camier, that we may admire it sink, below the horizon.

That long moment of brightness, said Mercier, with its thousand colours, always stirs my heart.

The day of toil is ended, said Camier, a kind of ink rises in the east and floods the sky.

The bell rang, announcing closing time.

I sense vague shadowy shapes, said Camier, they come and go with muffled cries.

I too have the feeling, said Mercier, we have not gone unobserved since morning.

Are we by any chance alone now? said Camier.

I see no one, said Mercier.

Let us then go together, said Camier.

They left the shelter.

The sack, said Mercier.

The umbrella, said Camier.

The raincoat, said Mercier.

It I have, said Camier.

Is there nothing else? said Mercier.

I see nothing else, said Camier.

I'll get them, said Mercier, you mind the bicycle.

It was a woman's bicycle, without free wheel unfortunately. To brake one pedalled backwards.

The ranger, his bunch of keys in his hand, watched them recede. Mercier held the handlebar, Camier the saddle. The pedals rose and fell.

He cursed them on their way.

II

In the show windows the lights came on, went out, according to the show. Through the slippery streets the crowd pressed on as towards some unquestioned goal. A strange well-being, wroth and weary, filled the air. Close the eyes and not a voice is heard, only the onward panting of the feet. In this throng silence they advanced as best they could, at the edge of the sidewalk, Mercier in front, his hand on the handlebar, Camier behind, his hand on the saddle, and the bicycle slithered in the gutter by their side.

You hinder me more than you help me, said Mercier.

I'm not trying to help you, said Camier, I'm trying to help myself.

Then all is well, said Mercier.

I'm cold, said Camier.

It was indeed cold.

It is indeed cold, said Mercier.

Where do our feet think they're taking us? said Camier.

They would seem to be heading for the canal, said Mercier.

Already? said Camier.

Perhaps we shall be tempted, said Mercier, to strike out along the towpath and follow it till boredom doth ensue. Before us, beckoning us on, without our having to lift our eyes, the dying tints we love so well.

Speak for yourself, said Camier.

The very water, said Mercier, will linger livid, which is not to be despised either. And then the whim, who knows, may take us to throw ourselves in.

The little bridges slip by, said Camier, ever fewer and farther between. We pore over the locks, trying to understand. From the barges made fast to the bank waft the watermen's voices, bidding us good night. Their day is done, they smoke a last pipe before turning in.

Every man for himself, said Mercier, and God for one and all.

The town lies far behind, said Camier. Little by little night overtakes us, blueblack. We splash through puddles left by the rain. It is no longer possible to advance. Retreat is equally out of the question.

He added, some moments later:

What are you musing on, Mercier?

On the horror of existence, confusedly, said Mercier.

What about a drink? said Camier.

I thought we had agreed to abstain, said Mercier, except in the event of accident, or indisposition. Does not that figure among our many conventions?

I don't call drink, said Camier, a quick nip to put some life in us.

They stopped at the first pub.

No bikes here, said the publican.

Perhaps after all he was a mere hireling.

And now? said Camier.

We might chain it to a lamppost, said Mercier.

That would give us more freedom, said Camier. He added, Of movement.

In the end they fell back on a railing. It came to the same.

And now? said Mercier.

Back to no bikes? said Camier.

Never! said Mercier.

Never say that, said Camier.

So they adjourned across the way.

Sitting at the bar they discoursed of this and that, brokenly, as was their custom. They spoke, fell silent, listened to each other, stopped listening, each as he fancied or as bidden from within. There were moments, minutes on end, when Camier lacked the strength to raise his glass to his mouth. Mercier was subject to the same failing. Then the less weak of the two gave the weaker to drink, inserting between his lips the rim of his glass. A press of sombre shaggy bulks hemmed them about, thicker and thicker as the hour wore on. From their conversation there emerged in spite of all, among other points, the following.

1. It would be useless, nay, madness, to venture any further for the moment.

2. They need only ask Helen to put them up for the night.

3. Nothing would prevent them from setting out on the morrow, hail, rain or shine, at the crack of dawn.

4. They had nothing to reproach themselves with.

5. Did what they were looking for exist?

6. What were they looking for?

7. There was no hurry.

8. All their judgements relating to the expedition called for revision, in tranquillity.

9. Only one thing mattered: depart.

10. To hell with it all anyway.

Back in the street they linked arms. After a few hundred yards Mercier drew Camier's attention to the fact that they were not in step.

You have your gait, said Camier, I have mine.

I'm not accusing anyone, said Mercier, but it's wearing. We advance in jerks.

I'd prefer you to ask me straight out, said Camier, straight out plump and plain, either to let go your arm and move away or else to fall in with your titubations.

Camier, Camier, said Mercier, squeezing his arm.

They came to a crossroads and stopped.

Which way do we drag ourselves now? said Camier.

Our situation is no ordinary one, said Mercier, I mean in relation to Helen's home, if I know where we are. For these different ways all lead there with equal success.

Then let us turn back, said Camier.

And lose ground we can ill afford? said Mercier.

We can't stay stuck here all night, said Camier, like a couple of clots.

Let us toss our umbrella, said Mercier. It will fall in a certain way, according to laws of which we know nothing. Then all we have to do is press forward in the designated direction.

The umbrella answered, Left! It resembled a great wounded bird, a great bird of ill omen shot down by hunters and awaiting quivering the coup de grâce. The likeness was striking. Camier picked it up and hung it from his pocket.

It is not broken, I trust, said Mercier.

Here their attention was drawn to a strange figure, that of a gentleman wearing, despite the rawness of the air, a simple frock-coat and top-hat. He seemed, for the moment, to be going their way, for their view was of his rear. His hands, in a gesture coquettishly demential, held high and wide apart the skirts of his cutaway. He advanced warily, with stiff and open tread.

Do you feel like singing? said Camier.

Not to my knowledge, said Mercier.

The rain was beginning again. But had it ever ceased?

Let us make haste, said Camier.

Why do you ask me that? said Mercier.

Camier seemed in no hurry to reply. Finally he said:

I hear singing.

They halted, the better to listen.

I hear nothing, said Mercier.

And yet you have good ears, said Camier, so far as I know.

Very fair, said Mercier.

Strange, said Camier.

Do you hear it still? said Mercier.

For all the world a mixed choir, said Camier.

Perhaps it's a delusion, said Mercier.

Possibly, said Camier.

Let's run, said Mercier.

They ran some little way in the dark and wet, without meeting a soul. When they had done running Mercier deplored the nice state, soaked to the buff, in which they would arrive at Helen's, to which in reply Camier described how they would immediately strip and put their things to dry, before the fire or in the hot-cupboard with the boiler and hot water pipes.

Come to think of it, said Mercier, why didn't we use our umbrella?

Camier looked at the umbrella, now in his hand. He had placed it there that he might run more freely.

We might have indeed, he said.

Why burden oneself with an umbrella, said Mercier, and not put it up as required?

Quite, said Camier.

Put it up now, in the name of God, said Mercier.

But Camier could not put it up.

Give it here, said Mercier.

But Mercier could not put it up either.

This was the moment chosen by the rain, acting on behalf of the universal malignity, to come down in buckets.

It's stuck, said Camier, don't strain it whatever you do.

Mercier used a nasty expression.

Meaning me? said Camier.

With both hands Mercier raised the umbrella high above his head and dashed it to the ground. He used another nasty expression. And to crown all, lifting to the sky his convulsed and streaming face, he said, As for thee, fuck thee.

Decidedly Mercier's grief, heroically contained since morning, could be no longer so.

Is it our little omniomni you are trying to abuse? said Camier. You should know better. It's he on the contrary fucks thee. Omniomni, the all-unfuckable.

Kindly leave Mrs. Mercier outside this discussion, said Mercier.

The mind has snapped, said Camier.

The first thing one noticed at Helen's was the carpet.

Will you look at that pile, said Camier.

Prime moquette, said Mercier.

Unbelievable, said Camier.

You'd think you never saw it till now, said Mercier, and you wallowing on it all these years.

I never did see it till now, said Camier, and now I can't forget it.

So one says, said Mercier.

If that evening the carpet in particular caught the eye, it was not alone in catching it, for a cockatoo caught it too. It clung shakily to its perch hung from a corner of the ceiling and dizzily rocked by conflicting swing and spin. It was wide awake, in spite of the late hour. Feebly and fitfully its breast rose and fell, faint quiverings ruffled up the down at every expiration. Every now and then the beak would gape and for what seemed whole seconds fishlike remain agape. Then the black spindle of the tongue was seen to stir. The eyes, averted from the light, filled with unspeakable bewilderment and distress, seemed all ears. Shivers of anguish rippled the plumage, blazing in ironic splendour. Beneath it, on the carpet, a great news-sheet was spread.

There's my bed and there's the couch, said Helen.

They're all yours, said Mercier. For my part I'll sleep with none.

A nice little suck-off, said Camier, not too prolonged, by all means, but nothing more.

Terminated, said Helen, the nice little suck-offs but nothing more.

I'll lie on the floor, said Mercier, and wait for dawn. Scenes and faces will unfold before my gaze, the rain on the skylight sound like claws and night rehearse its colours. The longing will take me to throw myself out of the window, but I'll master it. He repeated, in a roar, I'll master it!

Back in the street they wondered what they had done with the bicycle. The sack too had disappeared.

Did you see the polly? said Mercier.

Pretty thing, said Camier.

It groaned in the night, said Mercier.

Camier questioned this.

It will haunt me till my dying day, said Mercier.

I didn't know she had one, said Camier, what haunts me is the Kidderminster.

Nor I, said Mercier. She says she's had it for years.

She's lying of course, said Camier.

It was still raining. They took shelter in an archway, not knowing where to go.

When exactly did you notice the sack was gone? said Mercier.

This morning, said Camier, when I went to get my sulfamides.

I see no sign of the umbrella, said Mercier.

Camier inspected himself, stooping and spreading out his arms as if concerned with a button.

We must have left it at Helen's, he said.

My feeling is, said Mercier, that if we don't leave this town today we never shall. So let us think twice before we start trying to—.

He almost said recoup.

What exactly was there in the sack? said Camier.

Toilet requisites and necessaries, said Mercier.

Superfluous luxury, said Camier.

A few pairs of socks, said Mercier, and one of drawers.

God, said Camier.

Some eatables, said Mercier.

Rotten ripe for the muckheap, said Camier.

On condition we retrieve them, said Mercier.

Let us board the first express southward bound! cried Camier. He added, more soberly, And so not be tempted to get out at the nearest stop.

And why south, said Mercier, rather than north, or east, or west?

I prefer south, said Camier.

Is that sufficient ground? said Mercier.

It's the nearest terminus, said Camier.

True, said Mercier.

He went out into the street and looked up at the sky, a grey pall, look where he would.

The sky is uniformly leaden, he said, resuming his place under the arch, we'll drown like rats without the umbrella.

Camier criticized this simile.

Like rats, said Mercier.

Even if we had the umbrella, said Camier, we could not use it, for it is broken.

What fresh extravagance is this? said Mercier.

We broke it yesterday, said Camier. Your idea.

Mercier took his head between his hands. Little by little the scene came back to him. Proudly he drew himself up, to his full height.

Come, he said, regrets are vain.

We'll wear the raincoat turn and turn about, said Camier.

We'll be in the train, said Mercier, speeding south.

Through the streaming panes, said Camier, we try to number the cows, shivering pitiably in the scant shelter of the hedges. Rooks take wing, all dripping and bedraggled. But gradually the day lifts and we arrive in the brilliant sunlight of a glorious winter's afternoon. It seems like Monaco.

I don't seem to have eaten for forty-eight hours, said Mercier. And yet I am not hungry.

One must eat, said Camier. He went on to compare the stomach with the bladder.

Apropos, said Mercier, how is your cyst?

Dormant, said Camier, but under the surface mischief is brewing.

What will you do then? said Mercier.

I dread to think, said Camier.

I could just manage a cream puff, said Mercier.

Wait here, said Camier.

No no! cried Mercier. Don't leave me! Don't let us leave each other!

Camier left the archway and began to cross the street. Mercier called him back and an altercation ensued, too foolish to be recorded, so foolish was it.

Another would take umbrage, said Camier. Not I, all things considered. For I say to myself, The hour is grave and Mercier . . . well . . . He advanced towards Mercier who promptly recoiled. I was only going to embrace you, said Camier. I'll do it some other time, when you're less yourself, if I think of it.

He went out into the rain and disappeared. Alone in the archway Mercier began pacing to and fro, deep in bitter thought. It was their first separation since the morning of the day before. Raising suddenly his eyes, as from a vision no longer to be borne, he saw two children, a little boy and a little girl, standing gazing at him. They wore little black oilskins with hoods, identical, and the boy had a little satchel on his back. They held each other by the hand.

Papa! they said, with one voice or nearly.

Good evening, my children, said Mercier, get along with you now.

But they did not get along with them, no, but stood their ground, their little clasped hands lightly swinging back and forth. Finally the little girl drew hers away and advanced towards him they had addressed as papa. She stretched out her little arms towards him, as if to invite a kiss, or at least a caress. The little boy followed suit, with visible misgiving. Mercier raised his foot and dashed it against the pavement. Be off with you! he cried. He bore down on them, wildly gesturing and his face contorted. The children backed away to the sidewalk and there stood still again. Fuck off out of here! screamed Mercier. He flew at them in a fury and they took to their heels. But soon they halted and looked back. What they saw then must have impressed them strongly, for they ran on and bolted down the first sidestreet. As for the unfortunate Mercier, satisfied after a few minutes of fuming tenterhooks that the danger was past, he returned dripping to the archway and resumed his reflections, if not at the point where they had been interrupted, at least at one nearby.

Mercier's reflections were peculiar in this, that the same swell and surge swept through them all and cast the mind away, no matter where it embarked, on the same rocks invariably. They were perhaps not so much reflections as a dark torrent of brooding where past and future merged in a single flood and closed, over a present for ever absent. Ah well.

Here, said Camier, I hope you haven't been fretting.

Mercier extracted the cake from its paper wrapping and placed it on the palm of his hand. He bent forward and down till his nose was almost touching it and the eyes not far behind. He darted towards Camier, while still in this position, a sidelong look full of mistrust.

A cream horn, said Camier, the best I could find.

Mercier, still bent double, moved forward to the verge of the archway, where the light was better, and examined the cake again.

It's full of cream, said Camier.

Mercier slowly clenched his fist and the cake gushed between his fingers. The staring eyes filled with tears. Camier advanced to get a better view. The tears flowed, overflowed, all down the furrowed cheeks and vanished in the beard. The face remained unmoved. The eyes, still streaming and no doubt blinded, seemed intent on some object stirring on the ground.

If you didn't want it, said Camier, you had better given it to a dog, or to a child.

I'm in tears, said Mercier, don't intrude.

When the flow stopped Camier said:

Let me offer you our handkerchief.

There are days, said Mercier, one is born every minute. Then the world is full of shitty little Merciers. It's hell. Oh but to cease!

Enough, said Camier. You look like a capital S. Ninety if a day.

Would I were, said Mercier. He wiped his hand on the seat of his trousers. He said, I'll start crawling any minute.

I'm off, said Camier.

Leaving me to my fate, said Mercier. I knew it.

You know my little ways, said Camier.

No, said Mercier, but I was counting on your affection to help me serve my time.

I can help you, said Camier, I can't resurrect you.

Take me by the hand, said Mercier, and lead me far away from here. I'll trot along at your side like a little puppy dog, or a tiny tot. And the day will come—.

A terrible screech of brakes rent the air, followed by a scream and a resounding crash. Mercier and Camier made a rush (after a moment's hesitation) for the open street and were rewarded by the vision, soon hidden by a concourse of gapers, of a big fat woman writhing feebly on the ground. The disorder of her dress revealed an amazing mass of billowing underclothes, originally white in colour. Her lifeblood, streaming from one or more wounds, had already reached the gutter.

Ah, said Mercier, that's what I needed, I feel a new man already.

He was in fact transfigured.

Let this be a lesson to us, said Camier.

Meaning? said Mercier.

Never to despair, said Camier, or lose our faith in life.

Ah, said Mercier with relief, I was afraid you meant something else.

As they went their way an ambulance passed, speeding towards the scene of the mishap.

I beg your pardon? said Camier.

A crying shame, said Mercier.

I don't follow you, said Camier.

A six cylinder, said Mercier.

And what of it? said Camier.

And they talk about the petrol shortage, said Mercier.

There are perhaps more victims than one, said Camier.

It might be an infant child, said Mercier, for all they care.

The rain was falling gently, as from the fine rose of a watering pot. Mercier advanced with upturned face. Now and then he wiped it, with his free hand. He had not had a wash for some time.

Summary of two preceding chapters

I

Outset.

Meeting of Mercier and Camier.

Saint Ruth Square.

The beech.

The rain.

The shelter.

The dogs.

Distress of Camier.

The ranger.

The bicycle.

Words with the ranger.

Mercier and Camier confer.

Results of this conference.

Bright too late.

The bell.

Mercier and Camier set out.

II

The town at twilight.

Mercier and Camier on the way to the canal.

Vision of the canal.

The bicycle.

First bar.

Mercier and Camier confer.
Results of this conference.
Mercier and Camier on the way to Helen's.
Doubts as to the way.
The umbrella.
The man in the frockcoat.
The rain.
Camier hears singing.
Mercier and Camier run.
The umbrella.
The downpour.
Distress of Mercier.
At Helen's.
The cockatoo.
The Kidderminster.
The second day.
The rain.
Disappearance of sack, bicycle and umbrella.
The archway.
Mercier and Camier confer.
Results of this conference.
Departure of Camier.
Distress of Mercier.
Mercier and the children.
Return of Camier.
The cream horn.
Distress of Mercier.
The fat woman.
Mercier and Camier depart.
Rain on Mercier's face.

III

I trust an only child, I was born at P—. My parents came from Q—. It was from them I received, together with the treponema pallidum, the huge nose whose remains you have before you. They were severe with me, but just. For the least peccadillo my father beat me till I bled, with his solid razor-strop. But he never failed to notify my mother that she might dress my wounds, with tincture of iodine or permanganate of potash. Here lies no doubt the explanation of my unconfiding character and general surliness. Unfitted for the pursuit of knowledge I was taken away from school at the age of thirteen and placed with farmers nearby. Heaven, as they put it, having denied them offspring of their own, they fell back on me with very natural virulence. And when my parents perished, in a providential railway smash, they adopted me with all the forms and observances required by the law. But no less feeble of body than of mind I was for them a constant source of disappointment. To follow the plough, ply the scythe, flounder in the mangel-wurzels, and so on, were labours so far beyond my strength that I literally collapsed whenever forced to undertake them. Even as shepherd, cowherd, goatherd, pigherd, it was in vain I strained every nerve, I could never give satisfaction. For the animals strayed, unnoticed by me, into the neighbouring properties and there ate their bellyful of vegetables, fruit and flowers. I pass over in silence the combats between rutting males, when I fled in terror to take shelter in the nearest outhouse. Add to this that the flock or herd, because of my inability to count beyond ten, seldom came home at full muster, and with this too I was deservedly reproached. The only branches in which I may boast of having, if not excelled, at least succeeded, were the slaughter of little lambs, calves, kids and porklings and the emasculation of little bullocks, rams, billy goats and piglets, on condition of course they were still unspoiled, all innocence and trustingness. It was therefore to these specialities I confined myself, from the age of fifteen. I have still at home some charming little—well, comparatively little—ram's testes dating from that happy time. In the fowl-yard too I was a terror of accuracy and elegance. I had a way of smothering geese that was the admiration and envy of all. Oh I know you are listening with only half an ear, and that half unwilling, but that is nothing to me. For my life is behind me and my only pleasure left to summon up, out loud, the good old days happily gone for ever. At the age of twenty, or possibly nineteen, having been awkward enough to fecundate a milkmaid, I ran away, under cover of night, for I was closely watched. I improved this occasion by setting light to the barns, granaries and stables. But the flames were scarcely under way when they were doused by a downfall none could have foreseen, so starry was the sky at the moment of ignition. That was fifty years ago, feels like five hundred. He brandished his stick and brought it down with a thump on the seat which emitted instantaneously a cloud of fine ephemeral dust. Five hundred! he bellowed.

The train slowed down. Mercier and Camier exchanged a look. The train stopped.

Woe is us, said Mercier, we're in the slow and easy.

The train moved on.

We might have alit, said Mercier, now it's too late.

Next stop, said the old man, you alight with me.

This puts a fresh complexion on it, said Mercier.

Butcher's boy, said the old man, poulterer's boy, knacker's boy, undertaker's man, sexton, one corpse on top of another, there's my life for you. Gab was my salvation, every day a little more, a little better. The truth is I had that too in my bleeding blood, my father having sprung, with what alacrity you may imagine, from the loins of a parish priest, it was common knowledge. I infested the outlying whoreshops and saloons. Comrades, I said, having never learnt to write, comrades, Homer tells us, Iliad Book 3, lines 85 and following, in what consists happiness here below, that is to say happiness. Oh I gave it to them! *Potopompos scroton evohe!* Like that, hot and strong! Picked up at nightschool—he burst into a wild raucous laugh—free nightschool for glimmer-thirsty wrecks. Potopompos scroton evohe, the soft cock and buckets of the hard. Step out of here, I said, with a stout heart and your bollocks in your boots and come again tomorrow, tell the missus to go chase apes in hell. There were delicate moments. Then up I'd get, covered with blood and my rags in ribbons, and at 'em again. Brats the offscourings of fornication and God Almighty a cheap scent in a jakes. I cleaned myself up and crashed their weddings, funerals, balls, wakes and christenings. They made me welcome, another ten years and I'd be popular. I let them have it on the lot, hymen, vaseline, the evil day from dawn to dark. Till I came in for the farm, or better still the farms, for there were two. The creatures bless their hearts, they loved me to the end. A good job for me they did, for my snout was starting to crumble. People love you less when your snout starts to crumble.

The train slowed down. Mercier and Camier drew in their legs to let him pass. The train stopped.

Not alighting? said the old man. You're right, only the damned alight here.

He wore gaiters, a yellow block-hat and a rusty frock-coat reaching down to his knees. He lowered himself stiffly to the platform, turned, slammed the door and raised towards them his hideous face.

The train moved on.

Adieu adieu, cried Mr. Madden, they loved me to the end, they loved—.

Mercier, whose back was to the engine, saw him as he stood there, dead to the passengers hastening towards the exit, bow down his head till it lay on his hands at rest on the knob of his stick.

With what relief the eyes from this clutter to the empty sky, with what relief back again.

A fresh complexion, said Mercier, a totally fresh complexion.

Camier wiped the pane with the cuff of his sleeve caught between the palm and four crooked fingers.

It's the end, said Mercier, that just about—. He paused for thought. That just about finishes me, he said.

Visibility nil, said Camier.

You remain strangely calm, said Mercier. Am I right in thinking you took advantage of my condition to substitute this hearse for the express we agreed on?

Camier mumbled something about burnt bridges and indecent haste.

I knew it, said Mercier. I've been shamefully abused. I'd throw myself out of the window if I wasn't afraid I might sprain my ankle.

I'll explain everything, said Camier.

You'll explain nothing, said Mercier. You took advantage of my weakness to cod me I was getting on an express when in fact—. His face fell apart. More readily than Mercier's few faces fell apart. Words fail me, he said, to disguise what I feel.

But your weakness it was precisely, said Camier, that prompted this little subterfuge.

Explain yourself, said Mercier.

Seeing the state you were in, said Camier, it was imperative to go, and yet at the same time stay.

You are cheap, said Mercier.

We'll get down at the next stop, said Camier, and consider how to proceed. If we see fit to go on we'll go on. We'll have lost two hours. What are two hours?

I wouldn't like to say, said Mercier.

If on the other hand, said Camier, we see fitter to return to town—.

To town! cried Mercier.

To town, said Camier, to town we shall return.

But we have just come from town, said Mercier, and now you speak of returning there.

When we left town, said Camier, it was necessary to leave town. So we very properly left it. But we are not children and necessity has her whims. If having elected to drive us forth she now elects to drive us back shall we balk? I trust not.

The only necessity I know, said Mercier, is to get away from that hell as fast and as far as possible.

That remains to be seen, said Camier. Never trust the wind that swells your sails, it is always obsolete.

Mercier controlled himself.

A third and last possibility, said Camier, since none are to be neglected, is that we form the heroic resolution to stay where we are. In which case I have all we need.

A village just one long street, everything lined up in a row, dwellings, shops, bars, the two stations, railway and petrol, the two churches, graveyard and so on. A strait.

Take the raincoat, said Camier.

Pah I won't melt, said Mercier.

They entered an inn.

Wrong address, said the man. This is Messrs. Clappe and Sons, Wholesale Fruit and Vegetable Suppliers.

And what leads you to suppose, said Camier, that we have not business with father Clappe or one of his waste products?

They regained the street.

Is this an inn, said Camier, or is it the fish market?

This time the man made way, all of a flutter.

Come in, gentlemen, he said, step right in. It's not the Savoy, but it's . . . how shall I say? He took their measure with a quick furtive look. How shall I say? he said.

Say it, said Camier, and put us out of our pain.

It's . . . snug, said the man, there is no other word. Patrick! he cried. But there was another word, for he added, in a tone of tentative complicity, whatever that sounds like, It's . . . *gemütlich*.

He takes us for globe-trotters, said Mercier.

Ah, said the man, rubbing his hands, physiognomies—pronouncing as was his right the *g*—have no secrets for me. It's not every day that I have the honour . . . He hesitated. That I have the honour, he said. Patrick!

Speaking for myself, said Mercier, I am happy to meet you at last, you have been haunting me this long time.

Ah, said the man.

Yes sir, said Mercier. You appear to me most often on a threshold, or at a window. Behind you torrents of light and joy which should normally annihilate your features, but do not. You smile. Presumably you do not see me, across the alley from where you stand and plunged in deepest shadow. I too smile—and pass on. Do you see me, in my dreams, Mr. Gall?

Let me relieve you, said the man.

In any case it is a happiness to meet you again, said Mercier, in such happier circumstances.

Relieve us of what? said Camier.

Why, said the man, of your coats, your hats, how shall I say? Patrick!

But will you look at us, said Camier. Do we appear to be hatted? Are we wearing gloves, without our knowledge? Come sir!

A porter for our trunks, said Mercier, what are you waiting for?

Patrick! cried the man.

Vengeance! cried Mercier, taking a step forward.

It was fair day. The saloon was crowded with farmers, cattle-dealers and the like. The beasts proper were far on their way already, straggling along the miry backland roads, to the cries of the herds. Some would come at night to their familiar byres, others to others they knew not of. Bringing up the rear, behind the sodden ewes, a train of clattering carts. The herds held their pricks through the stuff of their pockets.

Mercier propped his elbows on the bar. Camier, on the contrary, leaned his back against it.

They guzzle with their hats on, he said.

Where is he now? said Mercier.

By the door, said Camier, observing us without appearing to do so.

Can one see his teeth? said Mercier.

His mouth is hidden behind his hand, said Camier.

I do not ask if his mouth is hidden, said Mercier, I ask if one can see his teeth.

One cannot see his teeth from here, said Camier, owing to the hand that hides them.

What are we doing here? said Mercier.

First eat, said Camier. Barman, what are your titbits today?

The barman rattled off a list.

Mine will be a button-fish salad, said Camier, with Dutch dressing.

Not on today, said the barman.

Then make it a hopper sandwich, said Camier.

Just finished the last, said the barman. He had heard it was better to humour them.

You keep a civil tongue in your head, said Mercier. He turned to Camier. What kind of a kip is this? he said. What kind of a trip is this?

At this point the journey of Mercier and Camier seemed likely indeed to founder. That it did not was doubtless due to Camier, mirror of magnanimity and ingenuity.

Mercier, he said, leave it to me.

Do something for God's sake, said Mercier, do something? Why must I always be the one to lead the way?

Call your employer, said Camier.

The barman seemed reluctant.

Call him, my good fellow, said Mercier, call him when you're told. Make the little sound he can tell from every other and would not fail to hear even in a howling gale. Or the little beck that is lost on all but him and would bring him running though the heavens were to fall.

But he whom Mercier had called Mr. Gall was already by their side.

Have I the honour of addressing the proprietor? said Camier.

I am the manager, said the manager, since he was the manager.

It appears there is no more hopper, said Mercier. You have a curious way of managing, for a manager. What have you done with your teeth? Is this what you call *gemütlich*?

The manager wore the air of one in thought. He had no taste for trouble. The extremities of his drooping grey moustache seemed bent on meeting. The barman watched him closely. Mercier was struck by the scant grey strands, fine as a babe's, trained forward with pitiable coquetry from the back of the head across the crown. Mr. Gall had never appeared to him thus, but always erect and smiling and radiant.

Ah well, said Mercier, no more about it, such shortage is understandable, after all.

Would you have a room by any chance, said Camier, where my friend might take a moment's rest? He is dropping with fatigue. He leaned towards the manager and whispered in his ear.

His mother? said the manager.

My mother is it? said Mercier. She died perpetrating me, the slut. Rather than meet my eye. What's all this? he said to Camier. Have you no respect for my family?

I could manage a room, said the manager, but of course—.

A moment's rest, said Camier, he is out on his feet.

Come on, nightmare pal, said Mercier, you can't refuse me that.

Of course at the full day rate, said the manager.

On an upper floor as far as possible, said Mercier, where I can throw myself out of the window without misgiving, should occasion arise.

You'll stick by him? said the manager.

To the last, said Camier.

Patrick! cried the manager. Where's Patrick? he said to the barman.

Out sick, said the barman.

What do you mean out sick? said the manager. I saw him last night. I even thought I saw him just now.

Out sick, said the barman. No hope they say. Sinking fast.

How aggravating, said the manager. What's the matter with him?

I do not know, said the barman.

And why was I not informed? said the manager.

We must have thought you knew, said the barman.

And who says it's serious? said the manager.

It's a rumour going the rounds, said the barman.

And where is he? said the manager. At home or—.

A pox on your Patrick! cried Mercier. Do you want to finish me?

Show the gentlemen up, said the manager. Take their order and hurry back.

Six? said the barman.

Or seven, said the manager. As the gentlemen prefer.

He watched them go. He poured himself a glass and tossed it off.

Ah Mr. Graves, he said, good day, what are you taking?

Nice pair, said Mr. Graves.

Oh that's nothing, said the manager, I'm used to it.

And where might I ask did you get used to it? said Mr. Graves in his incipient pastoral patriarch's thick bass. Not among us, I vow.

Where I got used to it? said the manager. He closed his eyes the better to see what was still in spite of all a little dear to him. Among my masters, he said.

I'm happy to hear you say so, said Mr. Graves. I wish you good day.

The manager capped this.

His weary gaze strayed over the saloon where the honourable yokels were making to depart. Mr. Graves had given the signal, they would not be slow to follow an example of such moment.

The barman reported back.

Mr. Gast did not at once reply, intent on the scene as it faded and gave way, before his open eyes, to a little grey medieval square where silent shapes, muffled up to the eyes, passed slowly with laboured tread in the deep snow.

They took both, said the barman.

Mr. Gast turned towards him.

They ordered a bottle of malt, said the barman.

Have they settled? said Mr. Gast.

Yes, said the barman.

Nothing else matters, said Mr. Gast.

I don't like the look of them at all, said the barman. Particular the long hank with the beard. The little fat one I wouldn't mind so much.

You keep out of it, said Mr. Gast.

He went and stood by the door to take civil leave of his customers whose departure, in a body, was now clearly imminent. Most of them climbed aboard old high-slung Fords, others dispersed through the village in search of bargains. Others gathered talking in the rain which did not seem to incommode them. They were perhaps so pleased, who knows, for professional reasons, to see it fall, that they were pleased to feel it fall, wetting them through. Soon they would be on their several ways, scattered along the muddy roads shadowy already in the last gleams of niggard day.

Each hastens towards his little kingdom, his waiting wife, his beasts snugly stalled, his dogs listening for the coming of their lord.

Mr. Gast returned to the saloon.

Have you served them? he said.

Yes, said the barman.

They made no remark? said Mr. Gast.

Only not to be disturbed, said the barman.

Where's Patrick? said Mr. Gast. At home or in hospital?

I think he's at home, said the barman, but I wouldn't vouch for it.

You don't know a great deal, said Mr. Gast.

I keep my mind on my work, said the barman. He fixed Mr. Gast in the eye. On my duties and prerogatives, he said.

You couldn't do better, said Mr. Gast, that way greatness lies. He went to the door. If I'm wanted, he said, I've gone out and won't be long.

He went out sure enough and sure enough was not long.

Dead, he said.

The barman wiped his hands in haste and crossed himself.

His last words, said Mr. Gast, before yielding up the ghost, were unintelligible. Not so his second last, a gem of their kind, namely, A pint, for the love of Christ, a pint.

What ailed him exactly? said the barman.

How many days had he coming to him? said the barman.

He drew on Saturday like the rest, said the barman.

Negligible so, said Mr. Gast. I'll send a sheaf.

A good pal as ever was, said the barman.

Mr. Gast shrugged his shoulders.

Where's Teresa? he said. Don't tell me she's been taken too. Teresa! he cried.

In the toilet, said the barman.

Nothing escapes you, said Mr. Gast.

Coming! cried Teresa.

A buxom wench appeared, a big tray under her arm and a clout in her hand.

Look at this sty, said Mr. Gast.

A man entered the saloon. He wore a cap, a trench-coat all tabs, flaps, pockets and leather buttons, riding-breeches and mountaineering boots. His still brawny back was bowed beneath a knapsack filled to bursting and he held a huge stick in his hand. He lurched across the saloon, dragging noisily his hobnailed soles.

Some are best limned at first sight, those liable to vanish and never reappear.

My parquet, said Mr. Gast.

Water, said Mr. Conaire (the name without delay).

Mr. Gast did not budge, nor did the barman. Had Mr. Gast budged, then doubtless the barman too had budged. But Mr. Gast not budging the barman did not budge either.

Water first, said Mr. Conaire, then floods of liquor. Thanks. Again. Thanks. Enough.

He shed his sack with convulsive contortions of shoulders and loins.

Gin, he said.

He took off his cap and shook it violently in all directions. Then he put it back on his shining sugarloaf.

You have before you, gentlemen, he said, a man. Make the most of it. I have footed it from the very core of the metropolitan gas-chamber without rest or pause except twice to—. He looked about him, saw Teresa (already seen, but now with ostentation), leaned across the bar and finished his phrase in a murmur. He looked from Mr. Gast to George (as the barman now is called), from George to Mr. Gast, as though to make sure his words had done their work. Then drawing himself up he declared in ringing tones, Little and often, little and often, and gently, gently, that's what I've come to. He leered at Teresa and broke into a strident laugh. Where's your convenience? he said, adding, Convenience! They call that a convenience!

Mr. Gast described the way that led to it.

What complications, said Mr. Conaire. Always the same abominable well-bred latency. In Frankfurt, when you get off the train, what is the first thing you see, in gigantic letters of fire? A single word: HIER. Gin.

Neat? said Mr. Gast.

Mr. Conaire stepped back and struck an attitude.

What age would you say I was? he said. He rotated slowly. Speak up, he said, don't spare me.

Mr. Gast named a figure.

Damnation, said Mr. Conaire, got it in one.

Tis the baldness is deceptive, said Mr. Gast.

Not another word, said Mr. Conaire. In the yard, did I hear you say?

At the back on the left, said Mr. Gast.

And to win from here to there? said Mr. Conaire.

Mr. Gast renewed his directions.

Lest I be taken short, said Mr. Conaire.

On his way out he paused for a brush with Teresa.

Hello sweety, he said.

Teresa eyed him.

Sir, she said.

What loveliness, said Mr. Conaire. At the door he turned. And graciousness, he said, what graciousness. He went out.

Mr. Gast and George exchanged a look. Get out your slate, said Mr. Gast. His next words were for Teresa. You couldn't be a little more endearing? he said.

The old dirt, said Teresa.

No one is asking you to wallow on the floor, said Mr. Gast. He began to pace up and down, then halted, his mind made up. Stop what you're doing, he said, and collect yourselves. I shall now treat of the guest, that wild lovable beast. A shame that Patrick is not here to hear me.

He threw back his head, clasped his hands behind him and treated of the guest. Even as he spoke he saw a little window opening on an empty place, a moor unbroken save for a single track, where no shade ever falls, winding out of sight its gentle alternate curves. Not a breath stirs the pale grey air. In the far distance here and there the seam of earth and sky exudes a sunflooded beyond. It seems an autumn afternoon, late November say. The little black mass slowly approaching gradually takes shape, a tilted wagon drawn by a black horse, without effort, saunteringly. The wagoner walks ahead, flourishing his whip. He wears a heavy greatcoat, light in colour, its skirts trailing on the ground. It may even be he is happy, for he sings as he goes, in snatches. Now and then he turns, no doubt to look inside. As he draws near he seems young, he lifts his head and smiles.

That will be all for today, said Mr. Gast. Impregnate yourselves with these considerations. They are the fruit of an eternity of public fawning and private snarls. I make you a present of them. If I'm wanted I'm out. Call me at six as usual.

There's something in what he says, said George.

There's men all over for you, said Teresa, no more ideal than a monkey.

Mr. Conaire reappeared, enchanted to have got it over so fast.

I had my work cut out, he said, but I did it, I did it. He shivered. Nice north pole you have here, he said, what will you take. Jump at the chance, I feel the other hell calling me back.

George jumped.

Your health, sir, he said.

Pledge it, pledge it, said Mr. Conaire, none deserves it more. And rosebud here, he said, would she deign to clink with us?

She's married, said George, and mother of three.

Fie upon you! cried Mr. Conaire. How can one say such things!

You're being stood a port, said George.

Teresa moved behind the bar.

When I think what it means, said Mr. Conaire. The torn flesh! The pretty crutch in tatters! The screams! The blood! The glair! The afterbirth! He put his hand before his eyes. The afterbirth! he groaned.

All the best, said Teresa.

Drink, drink, said Mr. Conaire, pay no heed to me. What an abomination! What an abomination!

He took away his hand and saw them smiling at him, as at a child.

Forgive me, he said, when I think of women I think of maidens, I can't help it. They have no hairs, they pee not neither do they cack.

Mention it not, said George.

I took you for a maiden, said Mr. Conaire, I give you my oath, no flattery intended. On the buxom side I grant you, nice and plump, plenty of bounce, a bosom in a thousand, a bottom in a million, thighs—. He broke off. No good, he said, not a stir out of him.

Teresa went back to her work.

I now come to the object of my visit, said Mr. Conaire. Would you happen to know of a man by the name of Camier?

No, said George.

Strange, said Mr. Conaire, seeing I was to meet him here, this very place, this very afternoon. Here's his card.

George read:

F. X. Camier
Private Investigator
Soul of Discretion

New one on me, said George.

Small and fat, said Mr. Conaire, red face, scant hair, four chins, protruding paunch, bandy legs, beady pig eyes.

There's a couple above, said George, showed up there a short time back.

What's the other like? said Mr. Conaire.

A big bony hank with a beard, said George, hardly able to stand, wicked expression.

That's him, cried Mr. Conaire, those are them! Slip up now and give him the word. Tell him Mr. Conaire is waiting in the lounge. Co-naire.

They left word not to be disturbed, said George. They'd turn on you like a shot, I tell you.

Listen, said Mr. Conaire.

George listened.

Well I don't mind trying, he said.

He went out and a moment later came back.

They're snoring, he said.

Rouse them, said Mr. Conaire.

The bottle is empty, said George, and there they are—.

What bottle? said Mr. Conaire.

They ordered a bottle of malt in the room, said George.

Oh the hogs, said Mr. Conaire.

There they are stretched out side by side in their clothes on the floor, said George. Snoring hand in hand.

Oh the hogs, said Mr. Conaire.

IV

The field lay spread before them. In it nothing grew, that is nothing of use to man. Nor was it clear at first sight what interest it could have for animals. Birds may have found the odd worm there. Its straggling expanse was bounded by a sickly hedge of old tree stumps and tangles of brambles perhaps good for a few bramble berries at bramble-berry time. Thistles and nettles, possible fodder at a pinch, contended for the soil with a sour blue grass. Beyond the hedge were other fields, similar in aspect, bounded by no less similar hedges. How did one get from one field to another? Through the hedges perhaps. Capriciously a goat, braced on its hind legs, its forefeet on a stump, was muzzling the brambles in search of the tenderer thorns. Now and then it turned with petulance away, took a few angry steps, stood still, then perhaps a little spring, straight up in the air, before returning to the hedge. Would it continue thus all round the field? Or weary first?

Some day someone would realize. Then the builders would come. Or a priest, with his sprinkler, and another acre would be God's. When prosperity returned.

Camier was reading in his notebook. He tore out the little leaves when read, crumpled them and threw them away. He watches me, he said, without a word. He drew a big envelope from his pocket, took from it and threw away the following: buttons, two specimens of head or body hair, an embroidered handkerchief, a number of laces (his speciality), one toothbrush, a strange piece of rubber, one garter, samples of material. The envelope too, when he had emptied it, he threw away. I might as well be picking my nose, he said, for all he cares. He rose, impelled by scruples that did him credit, and gathered up the crumpled leaves, those at least which the light morning breeze had not blown away, or hidden in a fold of the ground, or behind a clump of thistles. The leaves thus recovered he tore up and threw away. So, he said, I feel lighter now. He turned back towards Mercier. You're not sitting on the wet grass, I hope, he said.

I'm sitting on my half of our coat, said Mercier, clover is nothing to it.

Fine too early, said Camier, bad sign.

What is the weather doing, said Mercier, now you mention it.

Look and see, said Camier.

I'd rather you told me, said Mercier.

A pale raw blotch, said Camier, has appeared in the east, the sun presumably. Happily it is intermittent, thanks to a murk of tattered wrack driving from the west before its face. It is cold, but not yet raining.

Sit, said Mercier. I know you do not share my chilly nature, but profit by the bank just the same. Don't overdo it, Camier, a nice bloody fool I'd look if you caught pneumonia.

Camier sat.

Cuddle close, said Mercier, snug and warm. Now look, like me, wrap the slack round your legs. So. All we need now is the hard-boiled egg and bottle of pop.

I feel the damp creeping up my crack, said Camier.

So long as none creeps down, said Mercier.

I fear for my cyst, said Camier.

What you lack, said Mercier, is a sense of proportion.

I don't see the connexion, said Camier.

Just so, said Mercier, you never see the connexion. When you fear for your cyst think of your fistula. And when you tremble for your fistula consider your chancre. This method holds equally for what is called happiness. Take one for example entirely free from pain all over, both his body and the other yoke. Where can he turn for relief? Nothing simpler. To the thought of annihilation. Thus, whatever the conjuncture, nature bids us smile, if not laugh. And now, let us look things calmly in the face.

After a moment's silence Camier began to laugh. Mercier in due course was tickled too. Then they laughed long together, clutching each other by the shoulders so as not to collapse.

What innocent merriment, said Camier, finally.

Well you know what I mean, said Mercier.

Before going any further they asked and told each other how they felt. Then Mercier said:

What exactly did we decide? I remember we agreed, as indeed we always do, in the end, but I forgot as to what. But you must know, since it is your plan, is it not, we are putting into execution.

For me too, said Camier, certain details have faded, and certain refinements of reasoning. So if I have any light to throw it is rather on what we are going to do, or rather again on what we are going to try and do, than on why we are going to try and do it.

I'm ready to try anything, said Mercier, so long as I know what.

Well, said Camier, the idea is to return to town, at our leisure, and stay there for as long as necessary.

Necessary for what? said Mercier.

For retrieving our belongings, said Camier, or giving them up for lost.

It must indeed have been rich in refinements, said Mercier, the reasoning responsible for that.

It would seem to have seemed to us, said Camier, though I cannot swear to it, that the sack is the crux of the whole matter in that it contains, or did contain, certain objects we cannot dispense with.

But we have reviewed its entire contents, said Mercier, and deemed them superfluous without exception.

True, said Camier, and our conception of what is superfluous can scarcely have evolved since yesterday. Whence then our disquiet?

Well, whence? said Mercier.

From the intuition, said Camier, if I remember right, that the said sack contains something essential to our salvation.

But we know that is not so, said Mercier.

You know the faint imploring voice, said Camier, that drivels to us on and off of former lives?

I confuse it more and more, said Mercier, with the one that tries to cod me I'm not yet dead. But I take your meaning.

It would seem to be some such organ, said Camier, that for the past twenty-four hours has not ceased to murmur, The sack! Your sack! Our latest heart to heart made this quite clear.

I recall nothing of the kind, said Mercier.

And so the need for us, said Camier, if not to find, at least to look for it, and for the bicycle, and for the umbrella.

I fail to see why, said Mercier. Why not the sack alone, since our concern is with the sack alone.

I too fail to see why, said Camier, exactly why. All I know is that yesterday we did see why, exactly why.

When the cause eludes me, said Mercier, I begin to feel uneasy.

Here Camier was alone in wetting his trousers.

Mercier does not join in Camier's laugh? said Camier.

Not just this once, said Mercier.

This thing we think we need, said Camier, once in our possession and now no longer so, we situate in the sack, as in that which contains. But on further thought nothing proves it is not in the umbrella, or fastened to some part of the bicycle. All we know is we had it once and now no more. And even that we do not know for sure.

There's premises for you if you like, said Mercier.

It boils down then to some unknown, said Camier, which not only is not necessarily in the sack, but which perhaps no sack of this type could possibly accommodate, the bicycle itself for example, or the umbrella, or both. By what token shall we know the truth? By a heightened sense of well-being? Unlikely.

I had a strange dream last night, said Mercier, I was in a wood with my grandmother, she was—.

Most unlikely, said Camier. No, but perhaps rather a gradual feeling of relief, spun out in time, reaching its paroxysm a fortnight or three weeks later, without our knowing exactly to what it was due. An example of bliss in ignorance, bliss at having recovered an essential good, ignorance of its nature.

She was carrying her breasts in her hands, said Mercier, by the nipples held between finger and thumb. But unfortunately—.

Camier flew into a rage, into a feigned rage that is, for into a true rage with Mercier Camier could not fly. The former sat agape. Drops seemingly from nowhere glistened in the grey tangles of his beard. The fingers fumbled at the great bony nose, its red skin stretched to bursting, delved furtively in the black holes, spread to feel their way down the channelled cheeks, began again. The ashen eyes stared into space aghast. The brow, scored deep with aliform furrows due less to meditation than to chronic amaze, this brow was perhaps, all things considered, of this grotesque head the least grotesque feature. It culminated in an unbelievably tousled mass of dirty hair comprising every tone from tow to snow. The ears—no.

Mercier had little to say for himself.

You ask me to explain, said Camier, I do so and you don't mind me.

It's my dream came over me again, said Mercier.

Yes, said Camier, instead of minding me you tell me your dreams. And yet you know our covenant: no communication of dreams on any account. The same holds for quotes. No dreams or quotes at any price. He got up. Do you feel strong enough to move? he said.

No, said Mercier.

Camier go get you food, said Camier.

Go, said Mercier.

The stout little bandy legs carried him in no time to the village, from the waist up all swagger and swing, an act. Mercier, alone in the lee of the bank, wavered between his two familiar leanings, not knowing which way to fall. Was not the outcome the same? In the end he said, I am Mercier, alone, ill, in the cold, the wet, old, half mad, no way on, no way back. He eyed briefly, with nostalgia, the ghastly sky, the hideous earth. At your age, he said. Another act. Immaterial.

I was about to go, said Mr. Conaire, all hope abandoned.

George, said Camier, five sandwiches, four wrapped and one on the side. You see, he said, turning graciously to Mr. Conaire, I think of everything. For the one I eat here will give me the strength to get back with the four others.

Sophistry, said Mr. Conaire. You set off with your five, wrapped, feel faint, open up, take one out, eat, recuperate, push on with the others.

For all response Camier began to eat.

You'll spoil him, said Mr. Conaire. Yesterday cakes, today sandwiches, tomorrow crusts and Thursday stones.

Mustard, said Camier.

Before leaving me yesterday, said Mr. Conaire, for your matter of life and death, you appointed to meet me here, at this very place, that very afternoon. I arrive, ask George in what a state, with my invariable punctuality. I wait. Doubts gradually assail me. Can I have mistaken the place? The day? The hour? I unburden myself to the barman. I learn you are somewhere above-stairs, with your butty, for some time past what is more, the pair of you plunged in a crapulous stupor. I invoke the urgency of my business and request you be waked. No question. You are not to be disturbed, on any account. You entice me to this place and take measures to prevent my seeing you. I receive advice. Stay around, they'll soon be down. Weakly I stay. Are you soon down? Bah! I return to the charge. Wake him, tell him Mr. Conaire is below. What a hope! The guest's desires are sacred. I offer threats. They laugh in my face. I press my point. By force. They bar the way. By stealth, sneaking up the stairs. They overtake me. I go down on my knees. General hilarity. They egg me on to drink, to stay for dinner, to stay the night. I'll see you in the morning. I'll be told the moment you're down. The saloon fills. Labourers, travellers. I get carried away. I come to on a couch. It is seven in the morning. You are gone. Why was I not told? No one knew. What time did you leave? No one knows. Are you expected back? No one knows.

Camier raised an imaginary tankard, with flexed fingers to clinch his meaning. The real he emptied slowly at a single draught, then caught up his packet and went to the door. There he turned.

Mr. Conaire, he said, I present my apologies. There was a moment yesterday when you were much in my thoughts. Then suddenly pff! no longer, gone from them utterly. As if you had never been, Mr. Conaire.

No, that's not right, as if you had ceased to be. No, that's not right either, as if you were without my knowledge. Don't take what I say in evil part, Mr. Conaire, I have no wish to offend. The truth is I suddenly saw my work was over, I mean the work I am famous for, and that it was a mistake to have thought you might join me here, if only for a moment. I renew my apologies, Mr. Conaire, and bid you farewell.

And my bitch! cried Mr. Conaire.

Your old pet, said Camier. You miss her. You'd pay dear, what passes for dear, to get her back. You don't know when you're well off.

He went. Mr. Conaire half made to follow him. But for some time past he had been fighting the need. On his return from the yard he went to the street door and looked out, then turned back into the saloon where such sadness overcame him that he ordered more gin.

My little bitch! he groaned.

Come, come, said George, we'll get you another.

Queenie! groaned Mr. Conaire. Her smile was almost human!

One more out of the way, with any luck.

Mr. Gast was nowhere to be seen, and with good reason, for he was looking for snowdrops in a little wood, snowdrops for Patrick's sheaf.

Blow, blow, thou ill wind.

Teresa was nowhere to be seen either, without regret be it said, Teresa was nowhere to be seen.

Mercier would not eat. But Camier made him.

You are green, said Camier.

I think I'm going to be sick, said Mercier.

He was not mistaken. Camier held him up.

You'll feel better without it, said Camier.

And sure enough, little by little, Mercier did feel better, better than before being sick that is.

It's all the dark thoughts I've been revolving, said Mercier, ever since you went. I even wondered if you had abandoned me.

Leaving you the raincoat? said Camier.

There is every reason to abandon me, I know, said Mercier. He reflected a moment. It takes Camier not to abandon Mercier, he said.

Can you walk? said Camier.

I'll walk, never fear, said Mercier. He got up and took a few steps. How's that? he said.

The raincoat, said Camier, why not dump it? What good is it?

It retards the action of the rain, said Mercier.

A cerecloth, said Camier.

You go too far, said Mercier.

Do you want my honest opinion? said Camier. The one who has it on is no less to be pitied, physically and morally, than the one who has it off.

There's something in what you say, said Mercier.

They contemplated the raincoat where it lay spread out at the foot of the bank. It looked flayed. Flitters of chequered lining, its ghostly tartan rending to behold, still clung to the shoulders. A paler yellow marked those patches where the wet had not yet soaked through.

Let us be gone from here, said Camier.

Shall we not throw it away? said Mercier.

Let it lie where it is, said Camier, no needless exertion.

I should have liked to launch it, said Mercier.

Let it lie there, said Camier. Soon no trace of our bodies will subsist. Under the action of the sun it will shrivel, like dead leaf.

We could bury it, said Mercier.

Don't be mawkish, said Camier.

Otherwise someone will come and take it, said Mercier, some verminous brute.

What do we care? said Camier.

True, said Mercier, but we do.

Camier moved off. After a little Mercier came up with him.

You may lean on me, said Camier.

Not now, not now, said Mercier irritably.

What has you looking back all the time? said Camier.

It moved, said Mercier.

To wave, said Camier.

We didn't leave anything in the pockets by any chance? said Mercier.

Punched tickets of all sorts, said Camier, spent matches, scraps of newspaper bearing in their margins the obliterated traces of irrevocable rendezvous, the classic last tenth of pointless pencil, crumples of soiled bumf, a few porous condoms, dust. Life in short.

Nothing we'll be needing? said Mercier.

Did you not hear what I said? said Camier. Life.

They went a little way in silence, as every now and then it was their wont.

We'll take ten days if need be, said Camier.

No further transport? said Mercier.

What we seek is not necessarily behind the back of beyond, said Camier. So let our watchword be—.

Seek? said Mercier.

We are not faring for the love of faring, that I know of, said Camier. Cunts we may be, but not to that extent. He cast a cold eye on Mercier. Don't choke, he said. If you have anything to say, now speak.

I was thinking of saying something, said Mercier, but on second thoughts I'll keep it to myself.

Selfish pig, said Camier.

Go on you, said Mercier.

Where was I? said Camier.

Let our watchword be, said Mercier.

Ah yes, said Camier, lente, lente, and circumspection, with deviations to right and left and sudden reversals of course. Nor let us hesitate to halt, for days and even weeks on end. We have all life before us, all the fag end that is.

What's the weather like now, said Mercier, if I look up I'll fall down.

Like what it's always like, said Camier, with this slight difference, that we're beginning to get used to it.

I thought I felt drops on my cheeks, said Mercier.

Cheer up, said Camier, we are coming to the station of the damned, I can see the steeple.

God be praised, said Mercier, now we can get some rest.

Summary
of two preceding chapters

III

The train.
Madden interlude I.
The slow train.
Madden interlude conclusion.
The village.
The inn.
Mr. Gast.
The beasts on the roads.
The farmers.
Mercier's dream.
The journey in jeopardy.
Camier's presence of mind.
Patrick's illness.
Mercier and Camier mount.
Mr. Graves.
Patrick's death.
His second-last words.
Conaire interlude I.
Mr. Gast treats of the guest.
Mr. Gast's vision.
Conaire interlude II.
Mercier and Camier sleep.

IV

Next day.
The field.
The goat.
The dawn.
Mercier and Camier laugh.
Mercier and Camier confer.
Camier laughs alone.
Mercier's face.
Camier departs.
Mercier alone.
The inn.
Conaire interlude conclusion.
The snowdrops.
Mercier eats and vomits.
The raincoat.
They press on.
The steeple of the damned.

V

The day came at last when lo the town again, first the outskirts, then the centre. They had lost the notion of time, but all pointed to the Lord's Day, or day of rest, the streets, the sounds, the passers-by. Night was falling. They prowled about the centre, at a loss where to go. Finally, at the suggestion of Mercier, whose turn it must have been to lead, they went to Helen's. She was in bed, a trifle unwell, but rose none the less and let them in, not without having first cried, from behind the door, Who goes there? They told her all the latest, their hopes both shattered and forlorn. They described how they had been chased by the bull. She left the room and came back with the umbrella. Camier manipulated it at length. But it's in perfect trim, he said, quite perfect. I mended it, said Helen. Perhaps even if possible more perfect than before, said Camier. If possible perhaps, said Helen. It opens like a dream, said Camier, and when I release—click!—the catch it collapses unaided. I open, I close, one, two, click, plop, click, pl—. Have done, said Mercier, before you break it on us again. I'm a trifle unwell, said Helen. No better omen, said Camier. But the sack was nowhere to be seen. I don't see the parrot, said Mercier. I put it out in the country, said Helen. They passed a peaceful night, for them, without debauch of any kind. All next day they spent within doors. Time tending to drag, they manstuprated mildly, without fatigue. Before the blazing fire, in the twofold light of lamp and leaden day, they squirmed gently on the carpet, their naked bodies mingled, fingering and fondling with the languorous tact of hands arranging flowers, while the rain beat on the panes. How delicious that must have been! Towards evening Helen fetched up some vintage bottles and they drifted off contentedly to sleep. Men less tenacious might not have withstood the temptation to leave it at that. But the following afternoon found them in the street again, with no other thought than the goal they had assigned themselves. Only a few more hours and it would be night, nightfall, a few more leaden hours, so no time was to be lost. Yet even total darkness, total but for the streetlamps, so far from hindering their quest could only further it, all things considered. For the district they now aimed to get to, one to which they hardly knew the way, would be easier for them to get to by night than by day, since the one time they had got to it before, the one and only time, it had not been day, no, but night, nightfall. So they entered a bar, for it is in bars that the Merciers of this world, and the Camiers, find it least tedious to await the dark. For this they had another if less weighty reason, namely the advantage to be derived, on the mental level too, from immersion as complete as possible in that selfsame atmosphere which had so unsteadied their first steps. They set to therefore without delay. There is too much at stake, said Camier, for us to neglect the elementary precautions. Thus with a single stone they accounted for two birds, and even three. For they availed themselves of the respite to talk freely of this and that, with great profit, to themselves. For it is in bars that the Merciers of this heavenly planet, and the Camiers, talk with greatest freedom, greatest profit. Finally a great light bathed their understandings, flooding in particular the following concepts.

1. The lack of money is an evil. But it can turn to a good.
2. What is lost is lost.
3. The bicycle is a great good. But it can turn nasty, if ill employed.
4. There is food for thought in being down and out.
5. There are two needs: the need you have and the need to have it.
6. Intuition leads to many a folly.
7. That which the soul spews forth is never lost.
8. Pockets daily emptier of their last resources are enough to break the stoutest resolution.

9. The male trouser has got stuck in a rut, particularly the fly which should be transferred to the crotch and designed to open trapwise, permitting the testes, regardless of the whole sordid business of micturition, to take the air unobserved. The drawers should of course be transfigured in consequence.

10. Contrary to a prevalent opinion, there are places in nature from which God would appear to be absent.

11. What would one do without women? Explore other channels.

12. Soul: another four-letter word.

13. What can be said of life not already said? Many things. That its arse is a rotten shot, for example.

These illustrations did not blind them to the goal they had in view. This appeared to them, however, with ever increasing clarity as time wore on, one to be pursued with calm and collection. And being still just calm and collected enough to know they were no longer so they reached without difficulty the happy decision to postpone all action to the following day and even, if necessary, to the next but one. They returned then in excellent spirits to Helen's apartment and dropped asleep without further ceremony. And even the following day they refrained from the pretty frolics of wet forenoons, so keen were they to be on their toes for the trials to come.

It was chiming midday when they left the house. In the porch they paused.

Oh the pretty rainbow, said Camier.

The umbrella, said Mercier.

They exchanged a look. Camier vanished up the stairs. When he reappeared, with the umbrella, Mercier said:

You took your time.

Oh you know, said Camier, one does what one can. Are we to put it up?

Mercier scrutinized the sky.

What do you think? he said.

Camier left the shelter of the porch and submitted the sky to a thorough inspection, turning celtically to the north, the east, the south and finally the west, in that order.

Well? said Mercier.

Don't rush me, said Camier.

He advanced to the corner of the street, in order to reduce the risk of error. Finally he regained the porch and delivered his considered opinion.

In our shoes I wouldn't, he said.

And may one enquire why not? said Camier. It's coming down, if I am to believe my eyes. Can you not sense you're wet?

Your inclination would be to put it up? said Camier.

I don't say that, said Mercier, I simply ask myself when we'll put it up if we do not do so now.

To the unprejudiced eye it was less an umbrella than a parasol. From the tip of the spike to the ends of the stays or struts was a bare quarter of the total length. The stick was terminated by an amber knob with tassels. The material was red in colour, or had been, indeed still was in places. Shreds of fringe adorned the perimeter, at irregular intervals.

Look at it, said Camier. Take it in your hand. Come on, take it in your hand, it won't bite you.

Stand back! cried Mercier.

Where was it dug up at all? said Camier.

I bought it at Khan's, said Mercier, knowing we had only one raincoat to our name. He asked a shilling for it, I got it for eight pence. I thought he was going to embrace me.

It must have come out about 1900, said Camier. The year I believe of Ladysmith, on the Klip. Remember? Cloudless skies, garden parties daily. Life lay smiling before us. No hope was too high. We played at holding fort. We died like flies. Of hunger. Of cold. Of thirst. Of heat. Pom! Pom! The last rounds. Surrender! Never! We eat our dead. Drink our pee. Pom! Pom! Two more we didn't know we had. But what is that we hear? A clamour from the watch-tower! Dust on the horizon! The column at last! Our tongues are black. Hurrah none the less. Rah! Rah! A craking as of crows. A quartermaster dies of joy. We are saved. The century was two months old.

Look at it now, said Mercier.

A silence ensued which Camier was the first to violate.

Well, he said, do we put it up now or wait for the weather to worsen?

Mercier scrutinized the inscrutable sky.

Go take a look, he said, and see what you think.

Camier again gained the corner of the street. On his return he said:

There is perhaps a little light below the verge. Would you have me go up on the roof?

Mercier concentrated. Finally he exclaimed, impulsively:

Let us put it up and pray for the best.

But Camier could not put it up.

Give it here to me, said Mercier.

But Mercier had no better success. He brandished it above his head, but controlled himself in time.

What have we done to God? he said.

Denied him, said Camier.

Don't tell me he is all that rancorous, said Mercier.

Camier took the umbrella and vanished up the stairs.

No sooner was he alone than Mercier went. His path crossed, at a given moment, that of an old man of weird and wretched aspect, carrying under his arm what looked like a board folded in two. It seemed to Mercier he had seen him somewhere before and he wondered as he went on his way where that somewhere could have been. The old man too, on whom for a wonder the transit of Mercier had not been lost, was left with the impression of a scarecrow encountered elsewhere and busied himself for a space with trying to recall in what circumstances. So, as with laboured steps they drew apart, each occupied the other's thoughts in vain. But the least little thing halts the Merciers of this world, a murmur coming to its crest and breaking, a voice saying how strange the autumntide of day no matter what the season. A new beginning, but with no life in it, how could there be? More manifest in town than in the country, but in the country too, where slowly over the vast empty space the peasant seems to stray, so aimless that night must surely overtake him far from the village nowhere, the homestead nowhere to be seen. There is no time left and yet how it drags. Even the flowers seem past their time to close and a kind of panic seizes on the tired wings. The hawk stoops always too soon, the rooks rise from the fallows while it is still light and flock to their places of assembly, there to croak and squabble till nightfall. Then, too late, they agitate to set out again. Day is over long before it ends, man ready to drop long before the hour of rest. But not a word, evening is all fever, a scurrying to and fro to no avail. So short it is not worth their while beginning, too long for them not to begin, that is the time they are pent up in, as cruelly as Balue in his cage. Ask the hour of a passer-by and he'll throw it at you over his shoulder at a venture and hurry on. But you may be easy in your mind, he is not far wrong who every few minutes consults his watch, sets it by official astronomic time, makes his reckonings, wonders how on earth to fit in all he has to do before the endless day comes to an end. Or with furious weary gesture he gives the hour that besets him, the hour it always was and will be, one that to the beauties of too late unites the charms of prematurity, that of the Never! without more of an even dreader raven. But all day that is how it is, from the first tick to the last tack, or rather from the third to the antepenultimate, allowing for the time it needs, the tamtam within, to drum you back into the dream and drum you back out again. And in between all are heard, every millet grain that falls, you look behind and there you are, every day a little closer, all life a little closer. Joy in saltspoonfuls, like water when it's thirst you're dying of, and a bonny little agony homeopathically distilled, what more can you ask? A heart in the room of the heart? Come come. But ask on the contrary your way of the passer-by and he'll take your hand and lead you, by the warren's beauty-spots, to the very place. It's a great grey barracks of a building, unfinished, unfinishable, with two doors, for those who enter and for those who leave, and at the windows faces peering out. The more fool you to have asked.

Mercier's hand released the railing to which this attack of wind had fastened it. But he had not gone far when he stopped again to observe, advancing towards him, a ragged shaggy old man plodding along beside a donkey. The latter, unbridled, set with small steps its dainty dogged course beside the curb, unswervingly except to circumvent a stationary vehicle or a group of urchins at marbles on their hunkers in the gutter.

The man walked in the street, between the grey haunch and the hostile cars. They raised their eyes from the ground only when danger threatened, to take its measure. Mercier said to himself, disappointing again as usual, No outerness will ever disestablish that harmony. It was perhaps too great a call on his strength, this parting from Camier at so sombre an hour. Admittedly strength was needed for to stay with Camier, no less than for to stay with Mercier, but less than for the horrors of soliloquy. Yet there he is on his way again, the voice has ceased, he is over the worst of the old man and the donkey, his being fills again with that merciful fog which is the best he knows, he's good for the long road yet. His dim shape moves on, hugging the railing, in the shadow of God knows what evergreens so called, hollies perhaps, if shadow is the word for a light hardly less leaden than that of the bogland nearby. The collar of his coat is turned up, his right hand is in his left sleeve and vice versa, they lie jogging on his belly in senile abandon, now and then he glimpses as through shifting seaweed a foot dragging on a flagstone. Heavy chains, hung between small stone pillars, festoon with their massy garlands the pavement on the street side. Once in motion they swing on and on, steadily or with serpentine writhings. Here Mercier would come to play when he was small. Running along the line of chains he set them going, one after another, with a stick, then turned back to look how the great jolts shook the pavement from end to end till it seemed they would never come to rest.

VI

Camier sat near the door at a small red table with a thick glass top. On his left hand strangers were belittling equal strangers, while to his right the talk, in undertones, was of the interest taken by Jesuits in mundane matters. In this or some cognate connexion an article was cited, recently appeared in some ecclesiastical rag, on the subject of artificial insemination, the conclusion of which appeared to be that sin arose whenever the sperm was of non-marital origin. On this angelic sex issue was joined, several voices taking part.

Change the subject, said Camier, or I'll report you to the archbishop. You're putting thoughts in my head.

He could not distinguish clearly what lay before him, all outline blurred in the smoke-laden air. Here and there emerged, rifting the haze, the unanswerable gesture complete with irrefutable pipe, the conical hat, fragments of lower limbs and notably feet, shuffling and fidgeting from one state of torment to the next, as though the seat of the soul. But behind him he had the stout old wall, plain and bare, he could feel it in his rear, he laid the back of his head against it and rubbed. He said to himself, When Mercier comes, for come he will, I know my man, where will he sit? Here, at this table? This problem absorbed him for a time. No, he decided in the end, no, he must not, he Camier could not bear it, why he knew not. What then? The better to envisage this, that is to say what then, since Mercier must not join him in his corner, Camier took his hands from his pockets, disposed them before him on the table in a snug little heap and rested his face thereon, first gently, then with the full weight of the skull. And the vision was not long in coming of Camier seeing Mercier before Mercier Camier, rising and hastening to the door. There you are at last, he cries, I thought you had left me for ever, and he draws him to the bar-counter, or deep into the saloon, or they go out together, though this is hardly likely. For Mercier is weary, in want of rest and refreshment before going any further, and has things to tell that can ill brook delay, and Camier too has things to tell, yes, they have things of moment to tell each other and they are weary, they need to compose themselves, after this long separation, and take their bearings, determine more or less how they stand, whether the future is bright or dark or merely dim as so often, and if there is one direction rather than another in which preferably to bend their steps, in a word collect themselves sufficiently to press hotfoot on, all smiles and lucidity, towards one of the innumerable goals indulgent judgement equivails, or else all smiles (optional) do justice on this élan and admire them from a distance, one after another, for they are distant. It is then a glimpse is caught of what might have been were one not as one had to be and it is not every day such a hair is offered for splitting. For once whelped all over bar the howling. Having thus cleaned up the immediate future Camier raised his head and saw before him a creature which he took some little time, so great was the resemblance, to recognize as Mercier, whence a tangle of reflections that left him no peace (but what peace then!) till the next day but one, with the comforting conclusion that what he had so dreaded as to deem it unbearable was not to feel his friend by his side, but to see him cross the sill and tread the last stage of the great space separating them since noon.

Mercier's entry had provoked some embarrassment in the saloon, a kind of uneasy chill. And yet the company was of dockers and sailors for the most part, with a sprinkling of excisemen, such as are not easily affected, as a rule, by singularity of exterior. A hush fell none the less as voices lulled, gestures froze, tankards trembled tilted on the brink and all eyes looked the same way. An acute observer, had one been present, but none was, might well have been put in mind of a flock of sheep, or a herd of oxen, startled by some dark threat. Their bodies rigid, drawn with fixed glare to face the common foe, they are stiller for a moment than the ground on which they graze. Then all to their heels, or full tilt at the intruder (if weak), or back to whatever they were about, cropping, chewing, coupling, gambolling. Or in mind of those walking sick who still all speech where they pass, dispel the body and fill the soul with dread, pity, anger, mirth, disgust. Yes, when you outrage nature you need be mighty careful if you don't want to hear the view-halloo or suffer the succour of some repugnant hand. For a moment it seemed to Camier that things were going to turn nasty and his hamstrings tensed under the table. But little by little a vast sigh arose, an exhalation higher and higher like a shoreward sweeping wave whose might in the end collapses in froth and clatter, for the glee of children.

What became of you? said Camier.

Mercier raised his eyes, but their stare was not at Camier, nor even at the wall. What on earth could it have been that they fixed with such intensity? One wonders.

Christ what a face, said Camier, you look straight from the infernal regions. What's that you say?

No doubt about it, Mercier's lips had moved.

I know of only one, said Mercier.

They didn't beat you? said Camier.

Across them the shadow fell of a huge man. His apron ended halfway down his thighs. Camier looked at him, who looked at Mercier, who began to look at Camier. Thus were engendered, though no eyes met, images of extreme complexity enabling each to enjoy himself in three distinct simultaneous versions plus, on a more modest scale, the three versions of self enjoyed by each of the others, namely a total of nine images at first sight irreconcilable, not to mention the confusion of frustrated excitations jostling on the fringes of the field. In all a gruesome mess, but instructive, instructive. Add to this the many eyes fastened on the trio and a feeble idea may be obtained of what awaits him too smart not to know better, better than to leave his black cell and that harmless lunacy, faint flicker every other age or so, the consciousness of being, of having been.

What will it be? said the barman.

When we need you we'll tell you, said Camier.

What will it be? said the barman.

The same as before, said Mercier.

You haven't been served, said the barman.

The same as this gentleman, said Mercier.

The barman looked at Camier's empty glass.

I forget what it was, he said.

I too, said Camier.

I never knew, said Mercier.

Make an effort, said Camier.

You intimidate us, said Mercier, good for you.

We put a bold front on it, said Camier, though actually shitting with terror. Quick some sawdust, my good fellow.

And so on, each saying things he ought not to have said, till some kind of settlement was reached, sealed with sickly smiles and scurrilous civilities. The roar (of conversation) resumed.

Us, said Camier.

Mercier raised his glass.

I didn't mean that, said Camier.

Mercier set down his glass.

But why not, after all? said Camier.

So they raised their glasses and drank, both saying, at the same instant or almost, Here's to you. Camier added, And to the success of our—. But this was a toast he could not complete. Help me, he said.

I can think of no word, said Mercier, nor of any set of words, to express what we imagine we are trying to do.

Your hand, said Camier, your two hands.

What for? said Mercier.

To clasp in mine, said Camier.

The hands fumbled for one another beneath the table, found one another, clasped one another, one small between two big, one big between two small.

Yes, said Mercier.

What do you mean, yes? said Camier.

I beg your pardon, said Mercier.

You said yes, said Camier.

I said yes? said Mercier. I? Impossible. The last time I abused that term was at my wedding. To Toffana. The mother of my children. Mine own. Inalienable. Toffana. You never met her. She lives on. A tundish. Like fucking a quag. To think it was for this hectolitre of excrement I renegued my dearest dream. He paused coquettishly. But Camier was in no playful mood. So that Mercier resumed perforce, You are shy to ask me which. Then let me whisper it in your ear. That of leaving the species to get on as best it could without me.

I would have cherished a coloured baby, said Camier.

Ever since I favour the other form, said Mercier. One does what one can, but one can nothing. Only squirm and wriggle, to end up in the evening where you were in the morning. But! There's a vocable for you if you like! All is vox inanis save, certain days, certain conjunctions, such is Mercier's contribution to the squabble of the universals.

Where are our things? said Camier.

Where our umbrella? said Mercier.

As I was trying to help Helen, said Camier, my hand slipped.

Not another word, said Mercier.

I dumped it in the sluice, said Camier.

Let us go from here, said Mercier.

Where? said Camier.

Crooked ahead, said Mercier.

Our things? said Camier.

Less said the better, said Mercier.

You'll be my death, said Camier.

You want details? said Mercier.

Camier did not answer. Words fail him, said Mercier to himself.

You remember our bicycle? said Mercier.

Just, said Camier.

Speak up, said Mercier, I'm not deaf.

Yes, said Camier.

Of it there remains, said Mercier, securely chained to the railing, as much as may reasonably remain, after a week's incessant rain, of a bicycle relieved of both wheels, the saddle, the bell and the carrier. And the tail-light, he added, I nearly forgot. He struck his forehead a blow. What an addle-pate to be sure! he said.

And the pump of course, said Camier.

Believe it or not, said Mercier, it's all one to me, our pump has been spared.

And it such a fine pump, said Camier. Where is it?

Thinking it was a mere oversight, said Mercier, I left it where it was. It seemed the right thing to do. What is there for us to pump up now? That is to say I turned it upside down, I don't know why.

Does it fit as well so? said Camier.

Oh quite as well, said Mercier, quite, quite as well.

They went out. It was blowing.

Is it raining still? said Mercier.

Not for the moment, I fancy, said Camier.

And yet the air strikes damp, said Mercier.

If we have nothing to say, said Camier, let us say nothing.

We have things to say, said Mercier.

Then why don't we say them? said Camier.

We can't, said Mercier.

Then let us be silent, said Camier.

But we try, said Mercier.

We have got clear without mishap, said Camier, and unscathed.

What did I tell you? said Mercier. Continue.

We advance painfully—.

Painfully! cried Mercier.

Laboriously . . . laboriously through the dark streets, dark and comparatively deserted, because of the late hour no doubt, and the unsettled weather, not knowing who is leading, who following, whom.

By the ingle, said Mercier, snug and warm, they drowse away. Books fall from hands, heads on chests, flames die down, embers expire, dream steals from its lair towards its prey. But the watcher is on the watch, they wake and go to bed, thanking God for the position, dearly won, permitting of such joys, among so many others, such peace, while wind and rain lash against the panes and thought strays, spirit unalloyed, among those who have no refuge, the unable, the accursed, the weak, the unfortunate.

Do we as much as know, said Camier, what the other was up to all this time?

Again, said Mercier.

Camier repeated his remark.

Even side by side, said Mercier, as now, arm to arm, hand in hand, legs in unison, we are fraught with more events than could fit in a fat tome, two fat tomes, your fat tome and my fat tome. Whence no doubt our blessed sense of nothing, nothing to be done, nothing to be said. For man wearies in the end of trying to slake his drought at the fireman's hose and seeing his few remaining tapers, one after another, blasted by the oxyhydrogen blowpipe. So he gives himself over, once and for all, to thirsting in the dark. It's less nerve-rending. But forgive, there are days when fire and water invade my thoughts, and consequently my conversation, in so far as the two are connected.

I should like to ask some simple questions, said Camier.

Simple questions? said Mercier. Camier, you surprise me.

Their couching will be of the simplest, said Camier, all you have to do is reply without thinking.

If there's one thing I abominate, said Mercier, it's talking walking.

Our situation is desperate, said Camier.

Now now, said Mercier, none of your bombast. Would it be on account of the wind, do you suppose, that the rain has stopped, if it has?

Don't ask me, said Camier.

Let me tell you, said Mercier, before you go any further, I haven't an answer to my name. Oh there was a time I had, and none but the best, they were my only company, I even invented queries to go with them. But I sent them all packing long ago.

I don't mean that kind, said Camier.

And what kind so? said Mercier. This is looking up.

You'll see, said Camier. First, what news of the sack?

I hear nothing, said Mercier.

The sack, cried Camier, where is the sack?

Let's go down here, said Mercier, it's more sheltered.

They turned into a narrow street between high ancient houses.

Now, said Mercier.

Where is the sack? said Camier.

What possesses you to bring that up again? said Mercier.

You've told me nothing, said Camier.

Mercier stopped in his stride, which obliged Camier to stop in his too. Had not Mercier stopped in his stride, then Camier had not stopped in his either. But Mercier having stopped in his stride, Camier had to stop in his too.

Told you nothing? said Mercier.

Strictly nothing, said Camier.

What is there to tell, said Mercier, assuming I told you nothing?

Why, said Camier, if you found it, how things went, all that.

Mercier said, Let us resume our—. At a loss he gestured, with his free hand, towards his legs and those of his companion. There was a silence. Then they resumed that indescribable process not unconnected with their legs.

You were saying? said Mercier.

The sack, said Camier.

Would I appear to have it? said Mercier.

No, said Camier.

Well then? said Mercier.

So many things may have happened, said Camier. You may have looked for it, but in vain, found it and lost it again or even discarded it, said to yourself, It's not worth bothering about, or, Enough for today, tomorrow we'll see. How am I to know?

I looked for it in vain, said Mercier, longly, patiently, carefully, unsuccessfully.

He exaggerated.

Do I ask, said Mercier, how exactly you came to break the umbrella? Or what you went through before throwing it away? I combed innumerable sites, questioned innumerable parties, made allowance for the invisibility of things, the metamorphoses of time, the foible of folk in general, and of me in particular, for fabulation and fibbery, the wish to please and the urge to hurt, and had as well, just as well, stayed quietly where I was, no matter where, still trying to imagine against the endless approach, the shuffling slippers, the clinking keys, some better remedy than the yelp, the gasp, the whine, the skedaddle.

Camier said briefly what he thought of this.

Why do we insist, said Mercier, you and I for example, did you ever ask yourself that question, you who ask so many? Shall we fritter away what little is left of us in the tedium of flight and dreams of deliverance? Do you not inkle, like me, how you might adjust yourself to this preposterous penalty and placidly await the executioner, come to ratify you?

No, said Camier.

They held back on the brink of a great open space, a square perhaps, all tumult, fluttering gleams, writhing shadows.

Let us turn back, said Mercier. This street is charming. That brothel perfume.

They set about the street the other way. It seemed changed, even in the dark. Not they, or scarcely.

I see distant lands—, said Mercier.

Where are we going? said Camier.

Shall I never shake you off? said Mercier.

Do you not know where we are going? said Camier.

What does it matter, said Mercier, where we are going? We are going, that's enough.

No need to shout, said Camier.

We go wherever the flesh creeps least, said Mercier. We dodge along, hugging the walls, wherever the shit lies least thick. We stumble on an alley in a thousand, all we need do is pace it to and fro till it's no better than the others, and you want to know where we are going. Where are your sensibilities this evening, Camier?

I recapitulate, said Camier.

He did, then asked his simple questions. This brought them to the end of the alley where, as one man, they turned back yet again.

We talk too much, said Mercier. I have heard and said more inanities, since you took me in tow, than in all the rest of my life.

Tis I am in tow, said Camier. He added, The days of our talking together may well soon be ended. So let us think twice before we hold our tongue. For then you will turn to me in vain, and I to you, to me and you not there, but elsewhere, no better off, or barely.

What's all this? said Mercier.

So much so that I often wonder, said Camier, quite often, if we had not better part now, here and now, without more ado.

If it's my feelings you're appealing to, said Mercier, you should know better.

No later than today, for example, said Camier, I was on the point of not keeping our appointment.

So they had an appointment.

How strange, said Mercier, I had to wrestle with just such an angel.

One of us will yield in the end, said Camier.

Quite so, said Mercier, no need for both to succumb.

It would not be a desertion, said Camier, not necessarily.

Far from it, said Mercier, far from it.

By that I mean a forsaking, said Camier.

I took you to, said Mercier.

But the chances are it would, said Camier.

Would what? said Mercier.

Be one, said Camier.

Well obviously, said Mercier. To go on alone, left or leaver . . . Allow me to leave the thought unfinished.

They paced on a little way in silence. Then Mercier said:

I smell kips.

All is in darkness, said Camier. No light of any colour. No number.

Let us ask this worthy constable, said Mercier.

They accosted the constable.

Pardon, Inspector, said Mercier, would you by any chance happen to know of a house . . . how shall I say, a bawdy or brothelhouse, in the vicinity.

The constable looked them up and down.

Guaranteed clean, said Mercier, as far as possible, we have a horror of the pox, my friend and I.

Are you not ashamed of yourselves, at your age? said the constable.

What is that to you? said Camier.

Ashamed? said Mercier. Are you ashamed of yourself, Camier, at your age?

Move on, said the constable.

I note your number, said Camier.

Have you our pencil? said Mercier.

Sixteen sixty-five, said Camier. The year of the plague. Easy to remember.

Look you, said Mercier, to renounce venery because of a simple falling off in erotogenesis would be puerile, in our opinion. You would not have us live without love, Inspector, were it but once a month, the night of the first Saturday for example.

And that's where the taxpayers' good-looking money goes, said Camier.

You're arrested, said the constable.

What is the charge? said Camier.

Venal love is the only kind left to us, said Mercier. Passion and dalliance are reserved for blades like you.

And solitary enjoyment, said Camier.

The constable seized Camier's arm and screwed it.

Help, Mercier, said Camier.

Unhand him please, said Mercier.

Camier gave a scream of pain. For the constable, holding fast his arm with one hand the size of two, with the other had dealt him a violent smack. His interest was awakening. It was not every night a diversion of this quality broke the monotony of his beat. The profession had its silver lining, he had always said so. He unsheathed his truncheon. Come on with you now, he said, and no nonsense. With the hand that held the truncheon he drew a whistle from his pocket, for he was no less dexterous than powerful. But he had reckoned without Mercier (who can blame him?) and to his undoing, for Mercier raised his right foot (who could have foreseen it?) and launched it clumsily but with force among the testicles (to call a spade a spade) of the adversary (impossible to miss them). The constable dropped everything and fell howling with pain and nausea to the ground. Mercier himself lost his balance and came down cruelly on his hipbone. But Camier, beside himself with indignation, caught up the truncheon, sent the helmet flying with his boot and clubbed the defenceless skull with all his might, again and again, holding the truncheon with both hands. The howls ceased. Mercier rose to his feet. Help me! roared Camier. He tugged furiously at the cape, caught between the head and the cobbles. What do you want with that? said Mercier. Cover his gob, said Camier. They freed the cape and lowered it over the face. Then Camier resumed his blows. Enough, said Mercier, give me that blunt instrument. Camier dropped the truncheon and took to his heels. Wait, said Mercier. Camier halted. Mercier picked up the truncheon and dealt the muffled skull one moderate and attentive blow, just one. Like partly shelled hard-boiled egg, was his impression. Who knows, he mused, perhaps that was the finishing touch. He threw aside the truncheon and joined Camier, taking him by the arm. Look lively now, he said. On the edge of the square they were brought to a stand by the violence of the blast. Then slowly, head down, unsteadily, they pressed on through a tumult of shadow and clamour, stumbling on the cobbles strewn already with black boughs trailing grating before the wind or by little leaps and bounds as though on springs. On the far side debouched a narrow street the image of it they had just left.

He didn't hurt you badly, I hope, said Mercier.

The bastard, said Camier. Did you mark the mug?

This should greatly simplify matters, said Mercier.

And they talk of law and order, said Camier.

We would never have hit on it alone, said Mercier.

Best now go to Helen's, said Camier.

Indubitably, said Mercier.

Are you sure we were not seen? said Camier.

Chance knows how to handle it, said Mercier. Deep down I never counted but on her.

I don't see what difference it makes, said Camier.

You will, said Mercier. The flowers are in the vase and the flock back in the fold.

I don't understand, said Camier.

They went then mostly in silence the short way they had still to go, now exposed to the full fury of the wind, now through zones of calm, Mercier striving to grasp the full consequences for them of what had chanced, Camier to make sense of the phrase he had just heard. But they strove in vain, the one to conceive their good fortune, the other to arrive at a meaning, for they were weary, in need of sleep, buffeted by the wind, while in their skulls, to crown their discomfiture, a pelting of insatiable blows.

Summary
of two preceding chapters

V

Evening of the eighth (?) day.
At Helen's.
The umbrella.
Next day at Helen's.
Pastimes.
Next afternoon in the street.
The bar.
Mercier and Camier confer.
Result of this conference.
At Helen's.
Next day noon in front of Helen's.
The umbrella.
Looks at the sky.
The umbrella.
More looks at the sky.
Ladysmith.
The umbrella.
More looks at the sky.
The umbrella.
Mercier departs.
Mercier's encounters.
Mercier's mind.
The chains.

VI

Same evening.
Last bar but one.
Mother Church and artificial insemination.
The giant barman.
Mercier's contribution to the controversy of the universals.
The umbrella, end.
The bicycle, end.
In the street.
The ingle-nook.
The hose and the blowpipe.
The wind.
The fatal alley.
The sack.
The gulf.
The fatal alley.
Distant lands.
The fatal alley.
The constable.
The gulf.
"The flowers are in the vase."
The wind.
The endocranian blows.

VII

A road still carriageable climbs over the high moorland. It cuts across vast turfbogs, a thousand feet above sea-level, two thousand if you prefer. It leads to nothing any more. A few ruined forts, a few ruined dwellings. The sea is not far, just visible beyond the valleys dipping eastward, pale plinth as pale as the pale wall of sky. Tarns lie hidden in the folds of the moor, invisible from the road, reached by faint paths, under high overhanging crags. All seems flat, or gently undulating, and there at a stone's throw these high crags, all unsuspected by the wayfarer. Of granite what is more. In the west the chain is at its highest, its peaks exalt even the most downcast eyes, peaks commanding the vast champaign land, the celebrated pastures, the golden vale. Before the travellers, as far as eye can reach, the road winds on into the south, uphill, but imperceptibly. None ever pass this way but beauty-spot hogs and fanatical trampers. Under its heather mask the quag allures, with an allurement not all mortals can resist. Then it swallows them up or the mist comes down. The city is not far either, from certain points its lights can be seen by night, its light rather, and by day its haze. Even the piers of the harbour can be distinguished, on very clear days, of the two harbours, tiny arms in the glassy sea outflung, known flat, seen raised. And the islands and promontories, one has only to stop and turn at the right place, and of course by night the beacon lights, both flashing and revolving. It is here one would lie down, in a hollow bedded with dry heather, and fall asleep, for the last time, on an afternoon, in the sun, head down among the minute life of stems and bells, and fast fall asleep, fast farewell to charming things. It's a birdless sky, the odd raptor, no song. End of descriptive passage.

What is that cross? said Camier.

There they go again.

Planted in the bog, not far from the road, but too far for the inscription to be visible, a plain cross stood.

I once knew, said Mercier, but no longer.

I too once knew, said Camier, I'm almost sure.

But he was not quite sure.

It was the grave of a nationalist, brought here in the night by the enemy and executed, or perhaps only the corpse brought here, to be dumped. He was buried long after, with a minimum of formality. His name was Masse, perhaps Massey. No great store was set by him now, in patriotic circles. It was true he had done little for the cause. But he still had this monument. All that, and no doubt much more, Mercier and perhaps Camier had once known, and all forgotten.

How aggravating, said Camier.

Would you like to go and look? said Mercier.

And you? said Camier.

As you please, said Mercier.

They had cut themselves cudgels before leaving the timber-line. They made good headway, for their age. They wondered which would drop first. They went a good half mile without a word, no longer arm in arm, but each keeping to his side of the road whose whole width therefore, or nearly, lay between them. They opened their mouths simultaneously, Mercier to say, Strange impression sometimes—, and Camier, Do you think there are worms—?

Pardon, said Camier, what was that you said?

No no, said Mercier, you.

No no, said Camier, nothing of interest.

No matter, said Mercier, let's have it.

I assure you, said Camier.

I beg of you, said Mercier.

After you, said Camier.

I interrupted you, said Mercier.

I interrupted *you*, said Camier.

Silence fell again. Mercier broke it, or rather Camier.

Have you caught a chill? said Mercier.

For Camier had coughed.

It's a little early to be sure, said Camier.

I do hope it's nothing, said Mercier.

What a beautiful day, said Camier.

Is it not? said Mercier.

How beautiful the bog, said Camier.

Most beautiful, said Mercier.

Will you look at that heather, said Camier.

Mercier looked with ostentation at the heather and whistled incredulously.

Underneath there is turf, said Camier.

One would never think so, said Mercier.

Camier coughed again.

Do you think there are worms, said Camier, the same as in the earth.

Turf has remarkable properties, said Mercier.

But are there worms? said Camier.

Shall we dig a little hole and see? said Mercier.

Certainly not, said Camier, what an idea.

He coughed a third time.

The day was indeed fine, at least what passes for fine, in those parts, but cool, and night at hand.

Where shall we pass the night, said Camier, have we thought of that?

Strange impression, said Mercier, strange impression sometimes that we are not alone. You not?

I am not sure I understand, said Camier.

Now quick, now slow, that is Camier all over.

Like the presence of a third party, said Mercier. Enveloping us. I have felt it from the start. And I am anything but psychic.

Does it bother you? said Camier.

At first no, said Mercier.

And now? said Camier.

It begins to bother me a little, said Mercier.

Night was indeed at hand, and a good thing for them, without perhaps their yet admitting it, that night was at hand.

Hell, said Mercier, who the devil are you, Camier?

Me? said Camier. I am Camier, Francis Xavier.

I might well ask myself the same question, said Mercier.

Where do we plan to pass the night? said Camier. Under the stars?

There are ruins, said Mercier, or we can walk till we drop.

A little further on they did indeed come to the ruins of a house. A good half-century old by the look of them. It was almost night.

Now we must choose, said Mercier.

Between what? said Camier.

Ruin and collapse, said Mercier.

Could we not somehow combine them? said Camier.

We shall never make the next, said Mercier.

They walked on, if it could be called walking. Finally Mercier said:

I don't think I can go much further.

So soon? said Camier. What is it? The legs? The feet?

The head rather, said Mercier.

It was now night. The road vanished in darkness a few yards ahead of them. It was too early for the stars to give light. The moon would not rise till later. It was the darkest hour. They stood still, all but hidden from each other by the width of the road. Camier approached Mercier.

We'll turn back, said Camier. Lean on me.

It's my head, I tell you, said Mercier.

You see shapes that do not exist, said Camier. Groves, where none are. Strange animals loom, giant horses and cows, out of the murk do you but raise your head. High barns too and enormous ricks. And all more and more blurred and fuzzy, as if you were going blind before your very eyes.

Take me by the hand if you wish, said Mercier.

So hand in hand they retraced their steps, the big hand in the little, in silence. Finally Mercier said:

Your hand is clammy and you cough, perhaps you have senile tuberculosis.

Camier did not answer. They stumbled on. Finally Mercier said:

I hope we have not overstepped it.

Camier did not answer. There are times when the simplest words are slow to signify. Here "it" was the laggard. But do him justice, soon he called a sudden halt.

It's a little off the road, said Mercier, we may have passed it unawares, so black is the night.

One would have seen the track, said Camier.

So one would have thought, said Mercier.

Camier advanced, drawing Mercier in his wake.

Keep level with me for God's sake, said Camier.

Consider yourself fortunate, said Mercier, that you don't have to carry me. Lean on me, those were your words.

True, said Camier.

I decline, said Mercier, not wishing to be a burden. And when I lag a little you berate me.

Their progress was now no better than a totter. They overflowed on the bog, with risk of fatal consequences, to them, but nothing doing. Soon falls began to enter into play, now Camier accompanying Mercier (in his fall), now the reverse, and now the two collapsing simultaneously, as one man, without preconcertation and in perfect interindependency. They did not immediately rise, having practised in their youth the noble art, but rise in the end they did. And even at the worst moments their hands kept faith, although no knowing now which gave and which received the clasp, so confounded the confusion at this stage. Their anxiety (regarding the ruins) was no doubt in part to blame, and regrettably so, being ill-founded. For they came to them in the end, to those ruins they feared perhaps far behind them, they even had the strength to gain their inmost parts till these were all about them and they lay there as in a tomb. It was only then, sheltered from the cold they did not feel, from the unvexing damp, that they accepted rest, sleep rather, and that their hands were freed to go about their old business.

They sleep side by side, the deep doze of the old. They will speak together yet, but only at haphazard as the saying is. But did they ever speak together otherwise? In any case nothing is known for sure, henceforth. Here would be the place to make an end. After all it is the end. But there is still day, day after day, afterlife all life long, the dust of all that is dead and buried rising, eddying, settling, burying again. So let him wake, Mercier, Camier, no matter, Camier, Camier wakes, it's night, still night, he doesn't know the time, no matter, he gets up and moves away, in the dark, lies down again a little further on, still in the ruins, they are extensive. Why? No knowing. No knowing such things any more. Good reasons are never lacking for trying somewhere else, a little further on, a little further back. So good in the event that Mercier follows suit, at much the same moment no doubt. The whole question of priority, so luminous hitherto, is from now on obscure. There they are then lying, or perhaps merely crouching, at a reasonable remove from each other compared to their customary cleavings. They drowse off again, or perhaps simply lose themselves in thought. Before dawn in any case, well before, one of them gets up, say Mercier, fair is fair, and goes to look if Camier is still there, that is in the place where he thinks he left him, that is in the place where in the first instance they had dropped as one. Is that clear? But Camier is no longer there, how could he be? Then Mercier to himself, Well I never, the little rascal, he has stolen a march on me, and picks his way through the rubble, his eyes agoggle (for the least ray of light), his arms like antennae probing the air, his feet fumbling, gains and climbs the track leading to the road. Almost at the same moment, not precisely, that wouldn't work, almost, a little sooner, a little later, no importance, hardly any, Camier executes the same manoeuvre. The pig, he says, he has given me the slip, and gropes his way out with infinite precautions, life is so precious, pain so redoubtable, the old skin so slow to mend, out of this hospitable chaos, without a single word or other sign of gratitude, one does not return thanks to stone, one should. Such roughly must have been the course of events. There they are then back on the road, appreciably recruited in spite of all, and each knows the other is at hand, feels, believes, fears, hopes, denies he is at hand, and can do nothing about it.

Now and then they halt, all ears for the footfalls, footfalls distinguishable from all the other footfalls, and they are legion, softly falling on the face of the earth, more or less softly, day and night. But in the dark a man sees what is not, hears what is not, gives way to imaginings, there is no sense in giving heed, and yet God wot he does. So it may well be that one or the other stops, sits down on the side of the road, almost in the bog, to rest, or the better to think, or the better to stop thinking, good reasons are never lacking for coming to a stop, and that the other catches up, the one left behind, and seeing this kind of shade does not believe his eyes, at least not enough to run to its arms, or to kick it arse over tip into the quags. The sitter sees too, unless his eyes are closed, in any case he hears, unless he has gone to sleep, and taxes himself with hallucination, but half-heartedly. Then gradually he rises and the other sits, and so on, you see the gag, it can last them all the way to town, each yeaing and naying the other to no avail. For needless to say it is townward they are bound, as always when they leave it, as after long vain reckonings the head falls back among the data. But beyond the eastering valleys the sky changes, it's the foul old sun yet again, punctual as a hangman. Take a firm hold on yourselves now, we're going to see the glories of the earth once more, and on top of that ourselves once more, the night won't have made a ha'porth of difference, it's only the lid on the latrine, lucky we it has one, our brethren are there to dispel our hopes if any, our multitudinous brethren, and the rising gorge, and all the hoary old pangs. So there they are in view again, of each other, what less can you expect, they had only to set out sooner. Whose turn now, Camier's, then turn worm and have a good look. You can't believe your eyes, no matter, you will, for it's himself and no error, your boon old weary hairy skeleton of a butty, bet to the world, within stone's throw, but don't throw it, think of the good old days when you wallowed in the swill together. Mercier himself bows to the irrecusable, a habit one contracts among the axioms, while Camier raises his hand in a gesture at once prudent, courtly, elegant and uncompromising. Mercier hesitates an instant before acknowledging this salute, unexpected to say the least, which opportunity to hurry on Camier is not slow to seize. But even to the dead a man may wave, they do not benefit but the hearse squad are gratified, and the friends and relatives, and the horses, it helps them to believe they are surviving, the waver himself is the livelier for it too. Finally Mercier not at all put out raises in his turn his hand, not any old hand but the heterologous, in the affably selfless flourish prelates use when consecrating some portion of favoured matter. But to have done with these inanities, at the first fork Camier stopped and his heart beat fast with the thought of what to pack into a last long salute gravid to bursting with unprecedented delicacy. It was true countryside at last, quickset hedgerows, mud, liquid manure, rocks, wallows, cow-shit, hovels, and here and there a form unmistakably human scratching at his plot since the first scabs of dawn, or shifting his dung, with a spade, having lost his shovel and his fork being broken. A giant tree, jumble of black boughs, stands between the branching roads. The left leads straight to the town, at least what passes for straight in those parts, the second after long meandering through a rash of pestilential hamlets. Camier then, having reached this juncture, stopped and turned, whereon Mercier also stopped and half turned, all set to fly. But his fears were unfounded, for Camier merely raised his hand, in a gesture of salute similar in all respects to that with which he had already so kindly obliged, while darting the other, rigid at full stretch and doubtless quivering, at the right branch. A moment thus and then, with a kind of heroic precipitancy, he sprang off in the direction indicated and vanished, as into a burning house where three generations of his nearest and dearest were awaiting rescue. Reassured, but not entirely, Mercier advanced with caution to the fork, looked in the direction Camier had taken, saw no sign of him and hastened away in the other. Unstuck at last! Such roughly must have been the course of events. The earth dragged on into the light, the brief interminable light.

VIII

That's it. It takes a little time to grasp more or less what happened. It's your sole excuse, the best in any case. Enough to tempt you joking apart to have another go, another go at getting up, dressing up (paramount), ingesting, excreting, undressing up, dossing down, and all the other things too tedious to enumerate, in the long run too tedious, requiring to be done and suffered. No danger of losing interest, under these conditions. You cultivate your memory till it's passable, a treasure-bin, stroll in your crypt, unlit, return to the scenes, call back the old sounds (paramount), till you have the lot off pat and you all at a loss, head, nose, ears and the rest, what remains to snuff up, they all smell equally sweet, what old jingles to play back. Pretty beyond! And all that can still happen to you! Such things! Such adventures! You think you have done with it all and then one fine day, bang! full in the eye. Or in the arse, or in the balls, or in the cunt, no lack of targets, above all below the waist. And they talk of stiffs being bored!

It's wearing naturally, all-absorbing, no time left for putting a shine on the soul, but you can't have everything, the body in bits, the mind flayed alive and the archeus (in the stomach) as in the days of innocency, before the flop, yes, it's a fact, no time left for eternity.

But one black beast is hard to keep at bay, the waiting for the night that makes it all plain at last, for it is not every night possesses this property. This can drag on for months, the betwixt and between, the long dull mawkish muddle of regrets, the dead and buried with the undying, you've been through it all a thousand times, the old joke that has ceased to amuse, the smile unsmilable smiled a thousand times. It's night, fore-night, and there are no more sedatives. Fortunately it does not always last for ever, a few months do the trick as a rule, a few years, sudden ends have even been observed, in warm climates particularly. Nor is it of necessity unremitting, brief breaks for recreation are permitted, with the illusion of life they sometimes give, while they last, of time in motion, of a detail yet for the drain.

Then there are the pretty colours, expiring greens and yellows vaguely speaking, they pale to paler still but only the better to pierce you, will they ever die, yes, they will.

And to follow? That will be all, thank you. The bill.

Seen from outside it was a house like any other. Seen from inside too. And yet it emitted Camier. He still took the air in a small way, when the weather was fine. It was summer. Autumn would have suited better, late November, but there it is, it was summer. The sun was going down, the strings were tuning up, why God knows, before breaking into the old wail. Lightly attired Camier moved forward, his head resting on his breast-bone. Every now and then he straightened up, with a sudden jerk instantaneously annulled, by way of looking to see where he was going. He had felt even worse, he was in one of his better days. He got many a knock from the other foot-passengers, but not deliberate, they would all have preferred not to touch him. He was off for a little turn, no more, a little turn, he would very soon feel tired, very tired. Then he would halt, open wide his little blue-red eyes and cast about him till he had his bearings. Comparison of his strength with that required to get him home often drove him to the nearest bar for more, and for a little courage, a little courage and confidence regarding the way back, of which often too he had only the haziest notion. He helped himself on by means of a stick with which he struck the ground at every step he took, not at every two, at every one.

A hand landed with a thump on his shoulder. Camier froze, shrunk, but did not raise his head. He had no objection, it was even better thus, simpler, but not to the point of his losing sight of the earth. He heard the words, It's a small world. Fingers raised his chin. He saw a figure of towering stature, squalidly clad. No point in detailing him. He seemed well on in years. He stunk with the double stink of the old and the unwashed, that strongish smell. Camier inhaled it connoisseurishly.

Have you met my friend Mercier? said the man.

Camier looked in vain.

Behind you, said the man.

Camier turned. Mercier, apparently intent on a hatter's show-window, presented his profile.

Allow me, said the man. Mercier, Camier, Camier, Mercier.

They stood in the attitude of two blind men whom not unwillingness, but want of vision alone, prevents from growing acquainted.

I see you have met before, said the man. I knew it. Don't salute each other whatever you do.

I don't think I recognize you, sir, said Camier.

I am Watt, said Watt. As you say, I'm unrecognizable.

Watt? said Camier. The name means nothing to me.

I am not widely known, said Watt, true, but I shall be, one day. Not universally perhaps, my notoriety is not likely ever to penetrate to the denizens of Dublin's fair city, or of Cuq-Toulza.

Where did you make my acquaintance? said Camier. You must forgive my want of memory. I have not yet had time to unravel all.

In your moses basket, said Watt. You haven't changed.

Then you knew my mother, said Camier.

A saint, said Watt. She changed your diapers every two hours till you were pushing five. He turned to Mercier. Whereas yours, he said, I only saw inanimate.

I knew a poor man named Murphy, said Mercier, who had a look of you, only less battered of course. But he died ten years ago, in rather mysterious circumstances. They never found the body, can you imagine.

My dream, said Watt.

So he doesn't know you either? said Camier.

Come now, my children, said Watt, be on speaking terms again. Don't mind me. I'm discretion itself. The wild horse's despair.

Gentlemen, said Camier, allow me to leave you.

Were I not without desires, said Mercier, I would buy me one of those hats, to wear on my head.

Come have one on me, said Watt. He added, Chaps, with a smile devoid of malice, almost tender.

Really—, said Camier.

That fawn billycock on the block, said Mercier.

Watt took hold of Mercier's right arm, then, after a brief scuffle, of Camier's left, and drew them along.

Jesus off again, said Camier.

Mercier espied, in the far distance, the chains of his childhood, the same that had served him as playmates. Watt admonished him:

If you picked up your feet you'd make better progress. We're not going to have your teeth out today.

They advanced into the sunset (you can't deny yourself everything), burning up the sky higher than the highest roofs.

A pity Dumas the Elder cannot see us, said Watt.

Or one of the Evangelists, said Camier.

A different class, Mercier and Camier, for all their faults.

My strength is limited, said Camier, if yours is not.

We're nearly home, said Watt.

A police constable barred their way.

This is a sidewalk, he said, not a circus ring.

What is that to you? said Camier.

Fuck along with you now, said Mercier, and no nonsense.

Easy! Easy! said Watt. He stooped towards the constable. Inspector, he said, have a heart, they are a little—he tapped his forehead—but they wouldn't hurt a fly. The long hank takes himself for John the Baptist, of whom you have certainly heard, and Runty on my right daren't sit on his glass arse. As for me I am resigned to the utilities I was stuck with at birth, one of which consists in promenading these gentlemen, weather permitting. Given all this we can hardly be expected to form up in Indian file, as propriety requires.

Go and promenade in the country, said the constable.

We have tried, said Watt, time and time again. But they see red at the mere sight of green. Is that not curious? Whereas the shop-windows, concrete, cement, asphalt, neon, pickpockets, dogberries and kips, all this calms them down and sows in them the seeds of a night's refreshing sleep.

You don't own the sidewalk, said the constable.

Look out! cried Watt. See how their agitation grows! God grant they don't prove too much for me! He let go their arms and encircled their waists, hugging them against him. Forward my hearties, he said. They reeled off in a tangle of legs. The constable cursed them on their way.

What do you take us for? said Camier. Let me go.

But we're doing fine, said Watt. We smell of putrefaction one and all. Did you see his snout? He was dying for a snite. That's why he let us go.

They collapsed pell-mell in a bar. Mercier and Camier strained towards the counter, but Watt sat them down at a table and called for three doubles at the top of his voice.

Don't say you never put foot in this joint before, said Watt, I can well believe you. Order grappa and you're ejected.

The whiskey came.

I too have sought, said Watt, all on my own, only I thought I knew what. Can you beat that one? He raised his hands and passed them over his face, then slowly down his shoulders and front till they met again on his knees. Incredible but true, he said.

Disjointed members stirred in the grey air.

One shall be born, said Watt, one is born of us, who having nothing will wish for nothing, except to be left the nothing he hath.

Mercier and Camier paid scant heed to these sayings. They were beginning to look at each other again, with something of the old look.

I all but gave myself up, said Camier.

Did you return to the scene? said Mercier.

Watt rubbed his hands.

You do me good, he said, you really do me good. You almost comfort me.

Then I said to myself—, said Camier.

May you feel one day, said Watt, what now I feel. That won't prevent your having lived in vain, but it will, how shall I say—?

Then I said to myself, said Camier, that you might have had the same idea.

So you didn't, said Mercier.

A bit of warmth for the old cockles, said Watt, that's it, a touch of warmth for the poor old cockles.

I was afraid I might run into you, said Camier.

Watt banged the table, whereon an impressive silence fell. This was doubtless what he had in view, for into it he cast, in a voice crackling with vehemence:

Bugger life!

Indignant murmurs were heard. The manager approached, or perhaps even the proprietor. He was dressed with care. Some purists might have preferred, with his pearl-grey trousers, black shoes to the tan he wore. But after all he was on his own premises. By way of buttonhole he had chosen a tulip bud.

Out, he said.

Whence? said Camier. Hence?

Out to hell out of here, said the manager. It must have been the manager. But how different from Mr. Gast!

He has just lost his unique child, said Camier, unique of its kind.

Bigeminal, said Mercier.

His grief boils over, said Camier, could anything be more natural?

His wife is at her last, said Mercier.

We dare not let him out of our sight, said Camier.

One more small double, said Mercier, if we can prevail on him to swallow it he's saved.

None more dearly than he, said Camier, loves life, the humble daily round, the innocent pleasures and very pains themselves that permit us to supply the deficiencies of the Redemption. Make this clear to these good gentlemen. A cry of revolt has escaped him. His loss is so recent. Tomorrow, before his porridge, he will redden at the recollection.

He will wipe his lips, said Mercier, slip his napkin back into its ring, clasp his hands and ejaculate, Blessed be the dead that die!

Had he broken a glass, said Camier, we would be the first to reprove him. But such is not the case.

Overlook this little incident, said Mercier, it will not occur again. Will it, daddy?

Pass the sponge, said Camier, according to Saint Matthew.

And give us the same, said Mercier, your whiskey likes us.

Buy what did you say? said the manager, his cupidity aroused.

Geminal, said Camier.

Yes, said Mercier, everything double but the arse. We bury him day after tomorrow. Don't we, daddy?

It's the organizer made a balls of it, said Camier.

The organizer? said the manager.

Each egg has its little life and soul of the party, said Camier. Did you not know that? Sometimes he nods. Could you blame him?

Calm him down, said the manager. Don't try me too far.

He withdrew. He had been firm without harshness, human and yet dignified. He had not lost face before his customers, butchers for the most part, whom the blood of the lamb had made rather intolerant.

The second round came. The change from the first still lay on the table. Help yourself, my good man, said Camier.

The manager moved from group to group. Gradually the saloon revived.

How can one say such things? said Camier.

To think them is a crime in itself, said Mercier.

Towards man, said Camier.

And beast, said Mercier.

God alone would agree with him, said Camier.

That lot, said Mercier.

Watt seemed asleep. He had not touched his second glass.

Perhaps a sip of water, said Camier.

Let him be, said Mercier.

Mercier rose and went to the window. He introduced his head between the curtain and the glass, which enabled him, as he had foreseen, to observe the heaven. Its colours were not quite spent. He remarked at the same time, as he had not suspected, that from it a fine and no doubt gentle rain was dropping. The glass was not wet. He returned to his seat.

You know what often comes back to me? said Camier.

It's raining, said Mercier.

The goat, said Camier.

Mercier was looking perplexedly at Watt.

Day was breaking, said Camier, drizzly day.

Where have I seen this johnny before? said Mercier. He drew back his chair, crouched down and peered up at the face dim under the lee of the hat.

Old Madden too—, said Camier.

Suddenly Watt seized Camier's stick, wrenched it clear, raised it aloft and slammed it down in a passion of rage on the next table where a man with side-whiskers was sitting quietly reading his newspaper and smoking his pipe, before a foaming pint. What had to happen did, the glass top flew into smithers, the stick broke in two, the pint overturned and the man with side-whiskers intact fell over backwards, still sitting on the chair, the pipe in his mouth and the latest news in his hand. The piece of stick remaining in his Watt now hurled at the counter where it brought down a number of bottles and glasses. Watt waited for all the clatter and clash to subside, then bawled:

Fuck life!

Mercier and Camier, as though activated by a single wire, drained their glasses in haste and made a dash for the exit. Once safely there they turned. A stifled roar rose briefly above the hubbub:

Up Quin!

It's raining, said Camier.

I told you so, said Mercier.

Then farewell, said Camier.

You wouldn't walk with me a bit of the way? said Mercier.

What way? said Camier.

I live now beyond the canal, said Mercier.

It's not my way, said Camier.

There's a prospect there would break your heart, said Mercier.

Too late, said Camier.

We'll have a last one, said Mercier.

I haven't a make, said Camier.

Mercier put his hand in his pocket.

No, said Camier.

I've enough, said Mercier.

No I tell you, said Camier.

Like arctic flowers, said Mercier. In half an hour they'll be gone.

Canals mean nothing to me now, said Camier.

They advanced in silence to the end of the street.

Here I go right, said Mercier. He halted.

What ails you now? said Camier.

I halt, said Mercier.

They turned right, Camier on the sidewalk, Mercier in the gutter.

Up who? said Camier.

I heard Quin, said Mercier.

That must be someone who does not exist, said Camier.

The whiskey had helped after all. They made good headway, for their age. Camier missed his stick sorely.

I miss my stick, said Camier, it was my father's.

I never heard you speak of it, said Mercier.

Looking back on it, said Camier, we heard ourselves speaking of everything but ourselves.

We didn't bring it off, said Mercier, I grant you that. He took thought a moment, then uttered this fragment, Perhaps we might—.

What a deathtrap, said Camier, wasn't it here we lost the sack?

Not far from here, said Mercier.

Between the high ancient houses the pale strip of sky seemed even narrower than the street. It should on the contrary have seemed wider. Night plays these little tricks.

All . . . more or less nowadays? said Mercier.

Pardon? said Camier.

I ask if all is, you know, more or less, with you, nowadays.

No, said Camier.

A few minutes later tears welled up into his eyes. Old men weep quite readily, contrary to what one might have expected.

And you? said Camier.

Nor, said Mercier.

The houses grew fewer, the street broader, the sky more ample, they could see each other again, they had only to turn their heads, one to the left, the other to the right, only to raise their heads and turn them. Then suddenly all fell open before them, as if space had gaped and earth vanished in the shadow it casts skywards. But these are diversions do not last and they were not slow to be struck by their situation, that of two old men, one tall, one short, on a bridge. It itself was charming, connoisseurs were heard to say, a charming, charming bridge. Why not? Its name in any case was Lock Bridge, and rightly so, one had only to lean over the parapet to be satisfied on that score.

Here we are, said Mercier.

Here? said Camier.

The end went like magic, said Mercier.

And your prospect? said Camier.

Are you eyeless? said Mercier.

Camier scanned the various horizons, destrorsum, as always.

Don't rush me, he said, I'll try again.

You see it better from the bank, said Mercier.

Then why arse around up here? said Camier. Have you some sighs on your chest?

They went down on the bank. A bench with backrest was there to receive them. They sat.

So that's it, said Camier.

The rain fell silently on the canal, to Mercier's no little chagrin. But high above the horizon the clouds were fraying out in long black strands, fine as weepers' tresses. Nature at her most thoughtful.

I see our sister-convict Venus, said Camier, foundering in the skywrack. I hope it's not for that you dragged me here.

Further, further, said Mercier.

Camier screened his eyes with his hand.

Further north, said Mercier. North, I said, not south.

Wait, said Camier.

A little more, a little less.

Is that your flowers? said Camier.

Did you see? said Mercier.

I saw a few pale gleams, said Camier.

You need to have the knack, said Mercier.

I'd do better with my knuckle in my eye, said Camier.

The ancients' Blessed Isles, said Mercier.

They weren't hard to please, said Camier.

You wait, said Mercier, you only barely saw, but you'll never forget, you'll be back.

What is that grim pile? said Camier.

A hospital, said Mercier. Diseases of the skin.

The very thing for me, said Camier.

And mucous membrane, said Mercier. He cocked an ear. Not all that howling this evening.

It must be too early, said Camier.

Camier rose and went to the water.

Careful! said Mercier.

Camier returned to the bench.

Do you remember the parrot? said Mercier.

I remember the goat, said Camier.

I have the feeling he's dead, said Mercier.

We did not meet many animals, said Camier.

I have the feeling he was already dead the day she told us she had put him out in the country.

Waste no grief on him, said Camier.

He went a second time to the water, pored over it a little, then returned to the bench.

Well, he said, I must go. Farewell, Mercier.

Sleep sound, said Mercier.

Alone he watched the sky go out, dark deepen to its full. He kept his eyes on the engulfed horizon, for he knew from experience what last throes it was capable of. And in the dark he could hear better too, he could hear the sounds the long day had kept from him, human murmurs for example, and the rain on the water.

Summary
of two preceding chapters

VII

The bog.

The cross.

The ruins.

Mercier and Camier part.

The return.

VIII

The life of afterlife.

Camier alone.

Mercier and Watt.

Mercier, Camier and Watt.

The last policeman.

The last bar.

Mercier and Camier.

Lock Bridge.

The arctic flowers.

Mercier alone.

Dark at its full.